BRUTAL REALITIES

Colfax swung his feet off the desk and tossed the pencil down. He leaned across scattered papers and stared straight into Lew's eyes.

"You want some good advice, Zane? Don't try to be a detective. Don't jump to conclusions. Go on back home. If the sheriff over in Berryville thinks there's a case, he'll likely investigate real good and maybe he'll arrest somebody. Now, I'm busy and I don't do real good with gossip."

"You know damned well those two boys did what I say they did. They murdered my folks."

"Some more advice for you, Zane. You go messin' around with Wiley Pope and Fritz Canby and you're liable to wind up at the undertaker's yourself."

"Is that a threat?" Lew asked, rising from his chair.

"No threat, sonny boy. Just some good advice. You don't know what you're messin' with here. Those boys come from money and you ain't got a pot to piss in. So get on out of my office or I might have to lock you up for disturbin' the peace."

"What peace?"

"My peace," Colfax said, and his eyes turned to hard agates. The thin scrap of a smile on his face faded like smoke in a high wind.

THE VIGILANTE

Jory Sherman

BERKLEY BOOKS, NEW YORK

THE BERKLEY PUBLISHING GROUP
Published by the Penguin Group
Penguin Group (USA) Inc.
375 Hudson Street, New York, New York 10014, USA
Penguin Group (Canada), 90 Eglinton Avenue East, Suite 700, Toronto, Ontario M4P 2Y3, Canada
(a division of Pearson Penguin Canada Inc.)
Penguin Books Ltd., 80 Strand, London WC2R 0RL, England
Penguin Group Ireland, 25 St. Stephen's Green, Dublin 2, Ireland (a division of Penguin Books Ltd.)
Penguin Group (Australia), 250 Camberwell Road, Camberwell, Victoria 3124, Australia
(a division of Pearson Australia Group Pty. Ltd.)
Penguin Books India Pvt. Ltd., 11 Community Centre, Panchsheel Park, New Delhi—110 017, India
Penguin Group (NZ), Cnr. Airborne and Rosedale Roads, Albany, Auckland 1310, New Zealand
(a division of Pearson New Zealand Ltd.)
Penguin Books (South Africa) (Pty.) Ltd., 24 Sturdee Avenue, Rosebank, Johannesburg 2196,
South Africa

Penguin Books Ltd., Registered Offices: 80 Strand, London WC2R 0RL, England

This is a work of fiction. Names, characters, places, and incidents either are the product of the author's imagination or are used fictitiously, and any resemblance to actual persons, living or dead, business establishments, events, or locales is entirely coincidental.

THE VIGILANTE

A Berkley Book / published by arrangement with the author

PRINTING HISTORY
Berkley edition / October 2005

Copyright © 2005 by Jory Sherman.
Cover design by Erica Tricarico.
Cover illustration by John Paul.

ISBN: 0-425-20628-9

BERKLEY®
Berkley Books are published by The Berkley Publishing Group,
a division of Penguin Group (USA) Inc.,
375 Hudson Street, New York, New York 10014.
BERKLEY is a registered trademark of Penguin Group (USA) Inc.
The "B" design is a trademark belonging to Penguin Group (USA) Inc.

PRINTED IN THE UNITED STATES OF AMERICA

10   9   8   7   6   5   4   3   2   1

1

As always, the hills drew him into them, called to him through the soft sweet darkness before dawn in some silent siren song that only he could hear, first in some deep cavern of his heart, until it echoed in his waking brain like the haunting warble of a whippoorwill or the mournful flute of a mourning dove.

Lew Zane tiptoed through the log house, carrying his rifle, a .44/70-caliber Winchester '73. He had gone to sleep with his clothes on so that he would not make noise when he was ready to go. His parents were still sleeping and the house was quiet, except for the creaking of wood, the tick of the floors as they expanded and shrank with each shift in temperature. Sounds that were comforting during the night. He slipped some hardtack and cooked bacon into his pocket, the food wrapped in soft damp cloth the night before and kept in a tightly sealed tin. He felt something else in the tin, pulled it out, and felt its oilcloth wrapping. He smiled. His mother had made him a sandwich. He lifted the packet to his nostrils and sniffed the sourdough bread, the pickled cucumber, and squirrel meat. Sweet, sweet Ma, he thought, and slid the sandwich into his pocket.

He took a full canteen from a dowel on the wall and slung it over his shoulder, then walked out the back door, making sure that it did not slam shut behind him. He had oiled the metal hinges he had exchanged for the leather ones his father had made when he built the log house, and installed the mechanism that made the door close by itself. He had attached a small lead sash weight to a piece of wire, one end of which he screwed to the door, the other to the jamb. When the door opened, the weight lifted, and when someone walked in or out, the weight plunged downward and slid along the wire, pulling the door closed.

He stood on the back porch a minute, breathing deeply of the air. Then he heard sounds from inside the house and turned around. Footsteps and, through the window, he saw a faint orange glow. He pushed the door back open and stepped into the kitchen. His mother entered the kitchen, carrying a wooden lamp he had made for her. Inside, a candle burned, giving off a feeble light. Behind her, he saw the tall shape of his father. His mother was wrapped in her blue cotton robe; his father looked like a giant crimson sprite in his barn-red long underwear. Both were smiling as if they carried with them a secret they could not bear to keep any longer.

"I'm sorry," Lew said. "I didn't mean to wake you, Ma."

"Your pa and I wanted to wish you a happy birthday before you went out hunting," his mother said.

"Huh?"

"I'll bake you a cake after Pa and I get home from the store and I'll make candles for it."

"Nineteen of them," his father said, grinning.

"I forgot, I guess," Lew said.

"Oh, you mustn't forget your birthday, Lew," his mother said. "I remember the happy day you were born."

Lew blushed, feeling a warmth rush through him, like a fever burning through his veins as if he'd taken a shot of corn whiskey.

"I remember it too, son," his father said. "You bawled and squawked like a little Poland China piglet."

"Aw, come on, Pa. I was a good baby, wasn't I, Ma?"

"Not when you come out, you weren't," his father said. Then he walked over and tousled Lew's hair with a rustle of his fingers. "We just wanted to wish you a happy day before you set out, and invite you to come over to the store this evening when you finish hunting. We just might have a little surprise for you."

His mother stepped up and hugged her son. The smell of her hair washed over him like the perfume of honeysuckle and wisteria that grew over the trellis out front. Lew felt a tug at his heart that triggered a forgotten longing in him. He squeezed her with one arm, and she stretched up on her toes to plant a kiss on his forehead.

"Have a good hunt, Lew," she said. "Your daddy and I are going back to bed."

"I love you, Ma. You too, Pa." Lew was choked up, fighting back the tears welling up in his eyes. He did love them. And he knew they loved him too. They were the best parents a boy could have. They worked hard and never complained. Sometimes he wished they would complain so he wouldn't feel so guilty about his own whining when things went wrong.

"We love you, Lew," his mother said. "Be careful around that pond in the woods. I keep fearing you'll fall in someday and drown."

"Jenny," his father said, as if to keep her from going further with the thought that they all knew was in her mind.

"Oh, Del, I didn't mean anything by it. It's just that I worry, is all."

"I've got to get going," Lew said awkwardly. The lamplight glistened off the tears in his mother's eyes, and he knew his father was fighting back tears of his own. It had not been that long, he realized, and the hurt, the loss, was still with them.

"Go on with you, Lew," his father gruffed. "That big buck won't wait all day on you."

"Good-bye," Lew said, and turned back to the door. "Thanks for the sandwich, Ma."

"Good-bye," she said as he opened the door. He saw the lamp waver out of the corner of his eye, and then he was outside and he heard his parents' footsteps fade as they walked back down the hall to their bedroom.

There was still an inch or two of snow on the ground when he stepped off the porch and onto the ground. The paths and road were bare, however, and this would be the last day the snow would mantle the earth. It shone with an alabaster glow in the soft moonlight, and there was a bracing briskness to the air he breathed.

In the coolness, he could smell the cedars and the dead cornstalks still standing in the garden, the tentacles of rotting melon and cucumber vines, dead testaments to the end of winter.

As he walked toward the road that led up the long sloping hill behind the house, past the ermined garden, he felt as if he could hear the earth gestating, tugging at the fallen fibers of decaying plants, mixing them with the soil and the wetness, preparing for the spring that was soon to come. This had probably been their last snow, coming on the heels of March just before April began its magic of reincarnation, restoring the leaves and grass and greening the hills that rose around him into a verdant enchantment that never failed to amaze him and stir his blood. April, when the red buds would blossom and the slopes would sprout the white bright lights of the dogwood trees, so luminous in the green Eden of the Ozarks.

He did not go by the pond, but climbed to the top of the road and cut into the woods, following the ridge of a hollow where he had last seen the big ten-point buck the previous evening. Below, on the other side of the hollow, was the pond where the deer came to drink in the evenings and sometimes early in the morning before they left the hardwoods and went to their beds on the highest point of his property, next to the towering limestone bluffs that brooded over the valley beyond like ancient citadels gone to crag and ruin from the weather's slow and inexorable ravaging with wind and rain.

Lew wet his finger and tested the breeze, then walked slowly and quietly to a slab of rock that jutted out from the top of the hollow. The rock formed a table against a backdrop of earth and brush so that he presented no silhouette. The soft breeze drifted his way, across the pond below and up the hollow like a woman's intimate whisper in the darkness. He made no sound, and leaned against the dank loam of the bank behind him. The rock ledge was free of snow, but icy cold, sending a chill through his flesh clear to the marrow of his bones.

He sat there and listened as the dawn hovered in the east, beyond the creek and the Blue Hole, where he swam in summer with the local boys and girls of Osage, the little settlement some three miles from their farm. This was the land of the Osage, a tribe driven nearly to extinction not long after the first settlers arrived from Compton County, Tennessee, back in the 1830s. His parents had not been among that first group, but came later, down from Ohio and into Tennessee seeking kin, then following them to this long valley where Osage Creek flowed and wandered on its way to the Kings River.

A far-away whippoorwill blared its monotonous song, a leathery ribbon of notes that sounded like the whip of a razor strop in the stillness. The woods were still asleep, the squirrels snug in their winter dens, the turkeys roosting like boardinghouse drunks in the cedars and the walnut trees up by the bluffs, the rabbits in a stupor under rocks that kept them safe from the silent floating owls that prowled the night on feathery pinions that were almost soundless, no louder than the muffled breathing of a baby sleeping all swaddled in fur.

And then he heard the crack of a twig below his perch, the first sign of life in the somnolent forest. Lew did not move, but his senses shifted to a razor-sharp keen edge, sharp as a knife blade drawn across a honing stone until it could slice a single slender hair in twain with effortless ease.

The rifle lay across Lew's lap, a cartridge in the chamber, but the hammer still on half-cock. He touched the edge of the trigger, felt the chilling scimitar of its steel shape. He slipped his index finger inside the trigger guard, moved his thumb up to the hammer. When he cocked the rifle, he would squeeze gently on the trigger as he thumbed back the hammer so that, when the sear engaged in the lock, it would make no metallic click to warn the deer before he brought the rifle to his shoulder for the shot.

After the snap of the dry branch underfoot, the silence pounded like a tambour in Lew's ears. The silence rose up around him with the force of an ocean comber driven by a hurricane wind across an ominous green sea swelling in a silent rage beneath the froth beards of whitecaps. Lew strained his ears to listen, to pinpoint where the sound had come from and to try and detect where the animal, an animal large enough to break a thumb-thick twig, might be headed.

Pale cream light seeped through a rent in the dusky seam of the eastern sky. Gradually, the black of the night faded, leeching out all the bright stars on the horizon, letting the blue creep up the wall of sky until Venus winked out and the moon became a mere outline, like a memory, like the lingering smile of the Cheshire cat. Lew saw them then, the deer, moving through the hardwoods like ghosts, like oversized mice, the antlerless does slipping in and out of his vision as they climbed the steep slope of the ridge on the other side of the hollow.

Lew held his breath and waited. Puddles of shadow draped the snow at the feet of the trees, and the glistening crystals began to lose their luster. Objects that had been formless hulks in the night now took on definition, shape, became bushes, small saplings, stumps, rocks, hickory, walnut, and oak, stalwart among the fragrant cedars.

He saw the buck trailing some yards behind the half-dozen does, and Lew let out his breath in a slow exhalation. That was the ten-pointer, he thought, its head held high, his rack swinging first one way, then the other, his ears extended and twitching to pick up every scrap of sound.

With the exhalation of his breath, a strange thing happened, as it always seemed to happen when Lew was about to make a kill. A breeze sprang up from downwind, blowing toward him, whispering through the trees. It made a soft sighing sound and sent shivers up his spine. It made the hairs on his arms and the back of his neck stand up in stiff array, each one tingling like a tuning fork struck by a hammer. The does stopped and looked back down toward the bottom of the hollow. The buck stopped too, just for an instant as the wind made a soft moaning sound in the trees.

When the buck resumed walking, rustling the leaves with its hooves, Lew brought the rifle to his shoulder. He lined up the blade of the front sight with the slot in the buckhorn rear sight and put the muzzle on the deer's body just behind the right shoulder. The buck stopped and Lew drew a breath, held it as his finger curled around the trigger. He squeezed it gently and thumbed back the hammer on the lever-action rifle.

Lew thought of his father, wishing he were there with him to see the regal buck standing motionless between two trees, in full view. He squeezed the trigger, not knowing that he would never see his parents alive again.

2

THE TWO YOUNG MEN RODE DOWN FROM ALPENA, SOME thirteen miles, to the outskirts of Osage, the small town beyond Osage Creek that consisted of a school, a church, a dry-goods store, and a factory that made barrel staves. They did not cross over the bridge into town, but passed by the empty store a quarter mile before the bridge. They could see the church spire and the huge shape of the factory, the smaller boxlike shape of the single-room school. Folks had built the little school because the other one was on the other side of Osage Creek and the kids had to swim sometimes to get across since there was no bridge. The other school was still there, but only the biggest kids went there.

But the two young men's eyes were focused on the sign above the store by the side of the road, just above the creek. Snow glistened ghostly in the field beyond, desolate, empty, a night mirage suspended in the blackness of space. They slowed their horses and looked up at the sign over the store. They could read the legend, they were so close: DEL'S ROADSIDE STORE. Beneath the large block letters,

Fritz Canby made out the words DELBERT AND JENNIFER ZANE, PROPRIETORS. Elsewhere on the sign, in slanted print, they both saw the words PRODUCE, SUNDRIES, MEATS, LIQUOR.

"This the place?" Canby asked. "Says they got whiskey."

"I can read," Wiley Pope said. "Yep, this is it."

"It's awful quiet, ain't it?" Canby sniffled in the chill, his ferret eyes moving in their sockets like wooden beads rolling around in egg cups.

"It's supposed to be quiet, Fritz, you numbskull. That's why we come here at this ungodly hour, Chrissakes."

"I know that, Wiley, and don't you be callin' me no names, hear?"

"Just shut up. Let's ride around back and make sure."

"Make sure what?"

"They ain't nobody inside the store."

Pope led the way. They circled the store and rode close to the back. There was a door and a small back porch with no railings. There were some bins for trash and garbage on one side, both clean of snow, as was the porch. There was also a storage shed with a huge padlock on it, and several yards away, a smokehouse that reeked of curing pork and beef. It was also heavily padlocked, and ticked in the night like a railroad watch.

Pope reined his horse to a stop and studied the back door for several seconds. Wiley fidgeted, twirling his index finger in his horse's mane as if that would stop the shivers. He didn't know if he was shaking from fear or from the cold, but he realized this was a mighty big undertaking, and it was so quiet he could hear his heart pounding in his chest.

"Let's go," Pope said. "We'll tie up the horses a ways up the creek."

They rode down to the creek and back to the north. The creek, a small feeder creek that flowed into Osage Creek, gurgled as it flowed past them, racing with the energy of melted snow all along its banks. They came to a thicket of sumac and sarvis, their denuded branches skeletal tendrils that probed the night with bony fingers. Pope dismounted and tied his horse to one of the sarvis trees. He reached into his saddlebag and pulled out a canvas sack bulging with grain, a mixture of oats and cracked corn. He poured some of the contents onto the ground where the horse could reach it.

Canby tied up his horse to a sumac cluster a few yards away. Pope walked over and poured more grain, heaping it up into a mound. The horses began feeding.

"That'll keep 'em quiet," Pope said as he walked back to his horse and put the bag of grain back in his saddlebag. He pulled his pistol from its holster, a Colt .44 with rosewood grips. The barrel shone black in the moonlight. "Better check your pistol, Fritz."

"We ain't goin' to shoot nobody, are we?"

"Can't never tell, Fritz. We might."

"Hot damn. Maybe we better pull our bandannas over our faces."

"I swear, Fritz, if you ain't dumber'n a day-old pup sometimes. It's pitch-ass dark and they ain't nobody here and you want to play bank robber. It's just an old store run by two old grannies. If we can find that strongbox with the money I know they got in there, we'll be hootin' it up in Harrison this afternoon."

"How much money you figure they got, Wiley?"

"Maybe a couple thousand dollars."

Canby let out a low whistle, and Pope smacked him in back of the head to shut him up.

"Did you check your pistol, Fritz, like I told you?"

Canby pulled his pistol from its holster. It was a Smith & Wesson revolver, .38-caliber, with a four-inch barrel. Pope snorted when he saw it. "You maybe ought to buy you a man's gun with the money we get, Fritz. You got yourself a peashooter."

"My pap give it to me last year. Said it would drop a bear."

"Your pap is full of shit, Fritzie boy. You need yourself a genuine Colt .44."

"I'll get me one," Canby said, slipping his pistol back into his holster.

"Let's go. Real careful now," Pope said, and started toward the back porch of the store, gradually easing up the slope from the creek. Canby followed him, making all kinds of noise with his heavy work boots, slipping on slick snow and teetering at times like a boy walking a fence rail.

"Cripes, don't make so much noise," Pope said in a loud whisper. "You'll wake the damned dead."

There was a graveyard next to the church, but they couldn't see it. They both knew it was there, though, and both glanced uneasily in that direction. A water moccasin slithered from under a rock just ahead of Pope, and he watched it slide sideways down the slope, then plop into the creek.

"Oooweee, Fritz, did you see that sucker?"

"I saw it," Canby said. "Damned cottonmouths thick down in here."

"It liked to have bit me," Pope bragged.

Canby snorted in derision.

This was a lark for the two young men. They had planned it for a month or so, with Pope telling Canby about the strongbox the owners kept hidden inside, just stuffed with money. Pope delighted in seeing Canby's eyes widen and his lips go dry so that he licked them with his tongue. The robbery was a secret between them. Pope told Canby not to tell anyone what they were going to do, and Canby had agreed.

Pope stopped when he got to the back porch. He waited for Canby to catch up with him.

"Well, are we going in?" Canby asked.

"Just be quiet and listen for a damned minute, will you?"

They were quiet. They could barely hear the horses nibbling at the grain. Now they could see the graveyard, gleaming white under the snow and the moonlight. They both looked at it, then turned away. Both looked at the back door.

"How are we going to get in?" Canby whispered.

"Go get me one of them big rocks yonder," Pope said, pointing down the slope.

Canby scrambled down the slope and found a large round stone. He leaned down and pried it loose from the half-frozen ground. He grunted as he lifted it and carried it back up to the porch.

"Cripes, this must weigh ten pounds," Canby said, puffing slightly from the exertion.

Pope took the rock from Canby and put it up against the door, just beneath the latch. The rock was heavy, and he thought that was because melted snow water had probably seeped inside it. The rock was cold and damp and made his fingers numb.

"Need help?" Canby asked.

"Just hold on."

Pope shifted the rock in his hands for a better grip, pulled it away from the door, and then smashed it hard against the latch. The latch broke. Pope struck the door again in the same place and felt it give. He dropped the stone between his feet, panting from the exertion.

"Come on, Fritz. Now you can help me push the door in."

The two hit the door with their shoulders, and felt something splinter. The door gaped open, sagging against the top hinge. The bottom hinge broke away from the door, its screws wrenched from their holes.

Pope lunged inside the store, and was immediately disappointed that he found himself only in a small storeroom. But the shelves were crammed with goods, barely visible in the dim light from the moon and stars. Canby followed him inside, bumping into him.

"Watch where the hell you're going, Fritz."

"Geehaw, Wiley, it's black as a danged well in here."

"Come on." Pope opened a door and entered the store itself. He inhaled the scents that were so overpowering in the room after being out of doors. Hams and cured meats hung from rafter beams in one corner where there was a butcher table and display counter.

The two men wandered the aisles, gaping at the array of goods.

"I only been in here once," Pope said. "We were riding down to Springdale and Pa stopped in for some tea and he bought me candy."

"I never been here before, Wiley."

"Well, we got to be looking for that strongbox. You look behind those counters over there. I'll take the other side."

"We need to light us a lantern," Canby said. "I can't see my hands in front of my face."

"You dumb bastard," Pope whispered. "You light so much as a lucifer and folks will come running out here from town with scatterguns to blow us to kingdom come."

"Hell, I can't see nothing, Wiley."

"You know what a strongbox is, don't you?"

"I reckon."

"Well just feel around on the floor, on the shelves. It's got to be somewhere in here."

They roamed the store for almost an hour, but found no strongbox. Pope got down on his hands and knees, crawled every inch of the wall on one side of the store. Canby stretched to reach the top shelves and shook every likely box, or held it up close to his face when he was trying to read labels. Only a small amount of faint light sprayed in, like a mist, through the storefront windows. He crashed into a potbellied stove once, and stumbled over a stack of airtights on display in front.

His stomach growled with hunger when he found boxes of soda crackers.

"I'm hungry, Wiley."

"Damn, Fritz. Just help yourself. It's free, you know."

Finally, they searched the back storeroom while Fritz munched on dry crackers and dipped his finger into a jar of blueberry jelly. His mouth was smeared with the gelatinous substance so that he looked as if he had grown a light beard. In the light from outside, he looked like a raccoon, Pope thought.

"You ought to get you something to eat, Wiley."

"I'll eat after I find that damned money," Pope said.

Groping in the darkness on one of the shelves, Pope's hands bumped into something that clinked. Bottles. He ran his hands over them. They quavered and made a musical sound like someone tripping a finger across a bank of piano keys.

"Bottles," Pope murmured.

He pulled one of them off the shelf and examined it.

"Old Taylor," he said. "That's the kind of store-bought whiskey my pa drinks."

"Whiskey? You found you some whiskey, Wiley?"

"Damned right." Pope worried the cork out of the bottle and sniffed the heady aroma. "Yep," he said, "that's Old Taylor all right."

"Here, let me smell it," Canby said.

"Get your owned damned bottle. They's a whole shelf of it. This is mine." Pope lifted the neck of the bottle and placed it to his lips. He poured some into his mouth. It tasted like liquid fire.

Canby took a bottle of whiskey off the shelf.

The two boys eased down to the floor and sat, each with a whiskey bottle in his hands.

They began to drink while the sky paled in the east and the whippoorwills went silent. A pair of ducks flew overhead, heading away from Osage Creek to feed in the fields around Alpena. A mourning dove cooed from high in an oak tree, and the land began to light up like a magical stage set, with the snow glistening like billions of shattered diamonds.

3

THE BUCK JUMPED WHEN THE 150-GRAIN BULLET STRUCK IT just behind its right front leg. The soft lead pierced the hide, then smashed through muscle, bone, and sinew. By the time the bullet reached the heart, it had mushroomed into a flat chunk of lead that resembled a tiny hammerhead. The projectile burst through the heart and lodged against a bone in the rib cage. The deer bounded straight up in the air, then ran twenty yards, streaming blood from its still-pumping heart. It staggered another ten yards before its legs began to wobble beneath it. Then, with amazing energy, it struggled another ten yards, wobbled on the slope, and collapsed, mortally wounded. Its blood pumped another two or three seconds, then stopped. The deer lay still and its large eyes remained open, glazing over with the frosty breath of death.

Lew levered another cartridge into the chamber of his Winchester, then slid from the slab of rock and followed the blood trail. Bits of lung matter dotted the path the deer took, spongy particles as white as cuttlebone. The does had raced uphill at the shot, their tails bristling, flared like white fans. By the time Lew found the downed buck, the does had vanished, but he had marveled at their beauty as they bounded through the trees like African gazelles.

He prodded the fallen deer with the toe of his boot while pointing the muzzle of the cocked rifle at the animal, his finger caressing the trigger. But he knew the deer was dead, and he eased the hammer of the Winchester down to half-cock. He leaned down and lifted the deer's head by its antlers, marveling at their perfect formation, their symmetry. He sighed as he looked at the deer's glassy eyes, dulling in the morning light.

He knelt beside the deer and laid his rifle across its midsection. He looked up at the sky and spoke.

"Thank you, Father, for this food."

Then he looked back down at the deer.

"Thank you, my brother," he said. "You will feed my family and the grasses that grow from my grave will one day feed yours."

It was a moment of reverence his father had taught him.

"Always thank the Father of All, my son," Del had said. "And always thank the game you take. You must always respect life and the food on your table."

"Where did you learn this?" Lew had asked.

"From my father, who learned it from the Shawnee back in Ohio. The Indians lived much closer to nature than we do, and your grandfather thought it was a good thing to give thanks to the Almighty and to the game who gave up their lives so that we could live and survive."

His father and mother were not religious people, but he knew that they believed in God and tried to live by the Golden Rule. "Do unto others," they taught him, "as you would have them do unto you."

It should have been an easy rule to follow, but Lew was well aware of man's frailties and weaknesses. He did not always follow that rule, nor did he know anyone who did.

"Nobody's perfect," his mother had always said. "All you can do is try."

Lew stood up and drew out his knife, one given to him by his father on his sixteenth birthday. He kept it sharp. The knife had been made in Pennsylvania and was truly beautiful, with a blade etched in a hunting scene, a European stag running from hounds and a hunter carrying a flintlock, dressed in buckskins. The handle was carved out of rosewood and inlaid with brass. The rivets were made of iron.

He moved the rifle, laying it on a patch of ground he first cleared of snow. Then he turned the deer over so that its belly was exposed and made a slit from the vent to the chest cavity. He worked the knife easily, parting the flesh with the keen blade, a little at a time, until the body cavity was exposed. He reached around for a stick and propped the cavity open. He cut away the heart and liver, stuffed them inside his shirt. They were still warm and the warmth seeped through his long underwear into his flesh. He removed the entrails and set those aside.

He would let the deer cool before he took it down to the house and hung it up on a crossbar he had built for that purpose. There, he would skin it, keep the hide for tanning. He wiped his hands on his trousers, crabbed over to a tree, and leaned his back against it.

He set his canteen beside him, then took out the hardtack and bacon, began to nibble at the food as he gazed at the woods filling with a soft yellow light. He knew his father would be hitching up the buggy by then. Then he would bring it up to the house and call out Jenny's name. She would come out, still tying the strings of her bonnet, and ask why he had hitched up Pete, the mule, instead of Red Fox, the pretty horse. His father would say Pete liked the exercise and was more dependable than Red Fox. Red Fox, he would say, shied at every stump, clump, and clod. Very soon, though, they would be headed for the store, and they would not be home by the time he returned. They would welcome the meat to their larder, he knew, for they all had a taste for venison. He would have the meat cut up by the end of the day, and store most of it in the spring-house cut into a bank above the chicken house where the poke and the blackberries would soon be growing.

He might even have time to shoe one of their horses, the bay mare his mother sometimes rode when all three of them rode up to the bluffs or down to the Blue Hole. They owned some two thousand acres, and none of them had ever seen it all. There were two ponds, both stocked with bass and bluegill, and they raised a few head of cattle, grew hay for the winter. They were, he thought, blessedly self-sufficient. The store provided the small amount of cash they needed from time to time, and that was enough. They sold cattle, and had thought about raising hogs, but his mother said she could not abide the smell. They did not owe anything on their property, which they had bought for ten cents an acre some ten years ago.

It was an easy life, Lew admitted. He had no cows to milk, and his mother tended to the chickens and eggs. Lew was free to roam the hills and fish the streams, help with the calving and the haying. He could not complain, and he knew there were many who envied him. But he had learned from his mother and father to live with nature as much as possible.

"Just be what you are," his mother said. "Be what you do. Regard the lilies of the field."

He always laughed at that, but he saw the sense and wisdom in it. "They do not toil," his mother said. "They just grow and become what they are."

He supposed he should walk down to the pond. It was not far, and although he never told his folks about it, it was something he tried to do every day. His mother had mentioned her fear of him going there this morning, but he knew that wasn't the only reason she had mentioned it. Since that day, only three years ago, the memory of the pond was still painful to her. And she had not been back there since they had pulled little David out and prayed for life and breath to return to him.

The accident was tragic, but understandable in some ways. David would be fourteen now, had he lived. He was eleven when he and some other boys were fishing and swimming in the pond one summer. David was fishing at one end and the other boys were swimming at the other. They had taken one of Jenny's washtubs up there and grabbed an old whipsawed board out of the shed. They filled the tub with water from the pond and put it on one end of the board, while the other jutted over the pond, serving as a diving board. The boys had to take turns sitting in the tub of water so the others could dive off the springboard. It was a simple, yet effective creation, and the boys were proud of what they had done.

David had not been feeling well that day, and the other boys, Danny Slater, Kevin Smith, and Bobby Gleason, had teased him, splashing him with water as they swam by the bank where David was fishing.

The bank had turned slick and when David stood up, his feet slid from beneath him. He plunged into the water and didn't come up. The other boys dove down to look for him, but the water had been stirred up so much it was murky. They figured out later that David had gotten stomach cramps when he went into the water and couldn't swim back up to the surface and get help. It was a tragic drowning. No one blamed the other boys, but they blamed themselves. After the funeral, Lew never saw any of them again and nobody ever swam in their pond again.

Lew walked back up to where he had fired at the buck and looked around for the empty shell. When he saw it, he leaned down and picked it up, slipped it into his pocket. He finished munching on the hardtack and bacon, picked up his canteen, and washed the last of it down. He slung the wooden canteen over his shoulder and retrieved his rifle. Then he walked down to the pond while the deer cooled in the shade of the trees.

He ambled down to the pond, following the contours of the ridge on a slant. He heard a squirrel scamper down a tree, and knew they would all be out of their dens soon. The sun rose higher and in the open places, the snow was melting, nourishing the earth with its energy. Little trickles of water flowed from the melts, forming tiny rivers wending their way downhill where the ground was already saturated.

By nightfall, he knew, most of the snow would be gone and there would only be patches in the shadiest spots. By the next day, there wouldn't be a trace of winter anywhere to be seen.

The pond was beautiful at that time of morning, sleek and calm, as still and reflective as glass. He felt a lump in his throat as he looked at the place where David had lost his footing and fallen in. The marks were all gone now, but he remembered them well from that day when David had drowned. He could still see the slick mud, with twin grooves in it and the indentation where David had been sitting. His fishing pole had just been lying there where it had fallen, one end sticking in the water, little ripples still visible.

He had worked on David, trying to push the water out of his lungs and make him breathe again. Then his father had pushed and hammered on his chest with his fists. They had turned David over on his stomach. Water came out, but he did not draw a breath. His body made sounds that encouraged the boys standing by watching, but only angered Lew and brought tears to his father's eyes.

His pa had carried David back down to the house while Lew chased everyone away. His mother was waiting in the doorway at the back porch, and from the way David was lying in his father's embrace, legs and arms dangling, she knew her boy was dead.

He remembered her scream, how it had torn through him, ripping at the moorings of his heart, and he had heard that scream every time his mind went back to that terrible moment.

Lew stood there, up on the bank, looking down at the placid water, thinking of David and his mother. She had told Lew to be careful around the pond just that morning, and many times before. Well, what if he wasn't? he wondered. What if he just lost his footing, like David, and slid down into the water and never came up? For a fleeting moment he was tempted, but he knew it was only a loneliness gripping him, a sadness that was almost beyond comprehension, a longing to have his brother back with him, alive and smiling that smile of his, helping him with the deer he had shot.

He knew why his mother still worried about him. She had lost one son and did not want to lose another. Death was such a wrenching thing, he thought.

Death was such a sadness.

And, at that moment, Lew felt empty inside, as if the loss of his brother was only yesterday. The anger was gone but the sadness remained. And that horrible emptiness, deep inside his heart.

4

SHAFTS OF LIGHT STREAMED IN THROUGH THE FRONT windows of the store and a column of light, dancing with motes, collided with the darkness of the back room, with its door wide open. Pope and Canby were still ransacking the store, searching every nook and cranny for the strong-box that Pope insisted was hidden somewhere.

"It just ain't nowhere," Canby said, his voice slurred from the whiskey he had drunk. After the first couple of swallows he had done no more than sip on the liquor, but he was lightheaded from it. Canby had less tolerance for whiskey than Pope. Pope had stopped drinking to search for the money now that there was light in the store. His face was covered with dust and so were his hands, from brushing the top shelves of the store, searching vainly for anything that might contain money.

"It's somewhere, Fritz." Pope was angry by then, feeling that the storekeepers had cheated him, had somehow ruined his plan with their deceit. "And we're damned sure going to find it sooner or later."

"I hear something," Canby said as he jumped down from a stepladder he had placed against a wall of shelving.

The room went quiet as both listened.

"I hear it," Pope said.

He ran to the front of the store and, from one corner of the window, peered outside. By then he could hear the wheels of the buggy crunching the gravel of the road.

"Here comes the old geezer now," Pope said. "We got to hide."

Canby pressed up against Pope to look out the window.

"There's somebody with him," Canby said.

"You dumb cluck, that's his old lady. Now get."

Pope turned and shoved Canby away from him. The two scrambled away from the window. Pope ran behind the nearest counter. Canby stumbled over him as Pope squatted down. The two hunched there, their hearts pounding like trip-hammers in their chests. Both were a little drunk, but the excitement helped clear some of the fuzziness from their brains.

Pope pulled his pistol from its holster.

Canby put a hand on Pope's shoulder. His hand was trembling. "What you gonna do with that, Wiley?"

"I'm going to make 'em do what I tell 'em, Fritz. We're going to find out where they hid all their money."

Pope was a head taller than Canby, at a little under six feet. He was sandy-haired under his little felt hat, and he took it off now because he realized it was sticking up over the counter. Canby still had a few freckles sprinkled on his nose, but he was a year younger than Pope's eighteen. Canby was a gangly youth who looked up to Wiley as a big brother. He crowded close to Pope, who reached back and tried to swat him away.

"Don't crowd me, Fritzie."

"I'm backing you up, Wiley."

They listened, but could hear nothing at first. Then the sound of the buggy wheels became audible once again.

Now Pope himself was trembling too. But he was not afraid. He was just excited. At least that's what he told himself.

From where he squatted, Pope could see out the front window. He saw the buggy loom into view, circle on the road, then reappear again, facing the way it had come. The buggy stopped in front of the store and the woman stepped down. The two people outside said something to each other, but Pope couldn't hear what they said. He shrank back behind the counter, afraid one of them might see him.

When he peered out again, the woman was walking toward the store. She had a carpetbag slung over one arm. In her other hand, she had a key. She stepped onto the porch and came up to the door. Pope heard her slide the key into the tumbler lock and turn it. The door opened. He nearly jumped out of his skin when he heard the tinkle of the bell over the door. He had not noticed it before. It jangled until she closed the door behind her.

She started walking toward the back of the store, then froze. Pope held his breath. His fingers squeezed the grip of his pistol. He heard the buggy crunching away from the store, and then that sound stopped. He pictured the store-keeper parking the buggy and unhitching that old flea-bitten mule. Seconds passed like hours in his mind.

"Oh, dear," Jenny Zane said. "I'll bet Delbert forgot to close the back door."

Pope's heart pounded so hard he was sure she could hear it. Behind him, he heard Fritz stifle a sniffle. He wanted to strangle him.

"What's that?" Jenny said. Still, she did not move.

Pope's lips moved in a silent prayer. "Thank God. She's not coming over here."

Then Jenny started walking again, toward the store-room. Pope wondered if he should just let her go on and wait for her husband to enter the store.

But Pope heard her stop and turn around. She went to the front door and opened it to the jangling of the bell that made his skin jump. She stepped outside.

"Del, you must have left the back door open," she yelled.

Pope could not hear the gruff reply, but it sounded negative to him.

"Oh, yes, you did," Jenny hollered. "It's wide open and I think some critters got in the store."

"I'll be there in a minute," Del said, so loud even Pope and Canby heard him. Again, they held their breaths.

Jenny came back inside and closed the door. The bell clanged, and both boys felt its vibrations go right through to their bones.

Jenny's footsteps made a knocking sound on the hardwood flooring as she strode to the rear of the store. She paused at the storeroom door, and the boys heard her let out a gasp of surprise. Pope thought she had probably smelled the whiskey or seen the opened bottles. They had left them in plain sight on the floor.

Then Pope and Canby heard footsteps pounding on the front porch and a moment later, the door opened and that infernal bell pealed louder than before, it seemed.

Canby cursed in a loud whisper, and Pope knew the storekeeper had probably heard him. He had just enough courage from the whiskey to jump up and point his gun at Delbert Zane, who had stopped walking toward the back.

"Don't you make a damned move," Pope said as he came from behind the counter. The gun in his hand weighed a ton, and he saw his arm wave back and forth. His nerves screamed in his muscles and brain as if they had been galvanized by a lightning strike.

"What the hell is this?" Del said.

"Fritz, go fetch that woman and bring her in here," Pope ordered as he strode close to Del.

"You leave my wife alone."

"Shut up," Pope said.

Fritz ran to the back of the store, drawing his pistol from its holster.

"You, lady, come on."

"Oh, my," Jenny said, her face drained of color. Canby waved his pistol at her, and she scurried to her husband's side.

"You boys are in a lot of trouble," Del said.

"Just tell us where you keep the money," Pope said.

"What money?"

"The damned money in your strongbox, mister." Pope stepped closer. His hand was no longer shaking. Rage bloomed in his eyes like spewing lava from a black volcano.

"We don't have a strongbox," Del said. "There is no money."

"Damn you," Pope snarled. He raised his arm. Del cringed and started to back away. Jenny let out a startled cry of anguish. Pope brought his pistol down and struck Del in the face with the barrel. The blade's front side gouged open a furrow that began to bleed. Del's legs crumpled under him from the force of the blow and he dropped to his knees.

Jenny rushed to him and cradled his bleeding head in her hands. Tears gushed from her eyes.

"What have you done to him?" she shrieked.

"Lady," Pope said, "just tell us where you hide your money and you won't get hurt."

"We don't have any money," Jenny wailed.

"Don't you lie to me, lady," Pope said. "You'll wish you were dead."

"You little bastard," Del said, glaring up at Pope.

This enraged Pope even more.

"Don't you call me no names, mister," Pope said, balling up the fist that did not hold the pistol.

"Your daddy's a bastard and so are you," Del said.

"Del . . ." Jenny warned.

Pope's eyes flared with anger and he punched Del in the face, mashing his nose. Del recoiled from the impact. His eyes narrowed to slits and his jaw tightened.

"Please don't hit him anymore," Jenny begged. "I told you. We don't have any money here. Tell him, Del."

"She's not lying," Del said. "This isn't a bank. You can have what's in my pocket. That's all there is."

"Turn your pockets inside out," Pope commanded.

Del pulled a wad of paper money from his pocket, handed it to Pope. Pope counted it.

"There's only ten dollars here, mister." Pope stuffed the money in his pocket. Canby's eyes widened.

"That's all we have," Del said.

"Shit you say," Pope said, and swiped the barrel of his pistol across Del's face. They all heard a bone crack in Del's nose.

Jenny screamed, and this seemed to infuriate Pope even more. He stepped up to her and smashed the butt of his pistol square on her mouth. Blood gushed from her lips as if he had squashed a ripe tomato. Her cry of pain was garbled through the bubbles of blood that formed inside her mouth. Her teeth streamed red, giving her an addled look when she parted her lips.

"I want that fucking money," Pope said, his voice an animal snarl. "And lady, if one of you don't tell me where it is, I'm going to beat your husband to death right here and now."

"Leave her alone," Del said, trying to rise.

Canby stood by, gape-mouthed, excited at what Pope was doing without understanding why. His excitement was a light in his eyes that gave him the look of a madman; it was a swirl of feelings that made him lick his lips with a catlike slowness, as if he were a diner anticipating the next course at the dinner table.

Pope struck Del repeatedly in the face, slapping the barrel back and forth with a ferociousness that made Jenny recoil in horror. Blood streamed from Del's face where the skin had split open. His face looked like some hideous African mask, streamed as it was with blood and rips in the flesh from the front sight.

"The money, the money, the money," Pope kept saying over and over. "Give us the damned money, old man."

"Stop it," Jenny pleaded.

Pope struck Del again, this time with the butt of his pistol. The blow hit Del on top of the head and they all heard a crunch of bone. Blood gushed from a rent in Del's scalp, and his eyes rolled back in their sockets as he fell into a swoon.

Pope turned on Jenny as Del folded over at the waist and sat there hunched over, his breathing a wheeze in his throat, dry as a corn husk in November.

"You tell us, lady," Pope said, lifting his pistol to strike her.

She shrank back to avoid the blow, and brought a hand to her bloody lips. She looked at Del and wept.

"In—in the pantry floor," she gasped through sanguine teeth. "Sack of flour over a loose board. Oh, leave us alone. Please leave us alone."

"Fritz, go in that pantry back there and see if she's lying."

Canby stood stupefied for a minute, then turned on his heel and ran to the storeroom in the back as if he was glad to flee the scene of such brutality. Pope waited as Jenny put her arm over her husband's back and wept loudly, the tears flooding from her eyes and laving her face with a glistening wetness.

Pope heard noises and grunts from the back and he stood there, looking down at the helpless people huddled at his feet. It gave him a great feeling of power knowing that he had beaten them, that they had given up and were now just worthless lying folks who didn't deserve to live.

"I got it, I got it," Canby shouted, and ran back into the room, carrying an open box filled with a tangle of bills.

"Now leave us alone," Jenny said, her voice so soft it was barely audible.

Pope looked at the money as Canby thrust the box at him. His eyes flared with an obscene glow.

"Close the box, Fritz," Pope said.

Then he began to beat Del and Jenny to death before Canby's eyes. He beat them senseless and beyond death,

beat their faces until they were pudding or mashed pota-
toes, and he drooled spittle on them before he was finished.
His pistol was smeared with blood and so were his hands.
He wiped the pistol and his hands on Del's shirt, and then
kicked him in the stomach, flipping the dead man on his
back.

"Let's go," Canby whispered.

But Pope was oblivious to everything but the deaths he
had caused. His veins tingled with an electric charge, and
he let the feeling wash through him with its vivid heat until
it was a bright flower of pleasure in his brain that tasted
like strong whiskey and the scent of a woman in season.

5

LEW WAS IN THE BARN WHEN HE HEARD HOOFBEATS POUNDING up the road. He had just finished tacking the last nail in the last horseshoe on the hoof of Rose, his mother's bay mare. The buck he had shot that morning was skinned and butchered, the meat put away in the springhouse, except for a portion of the hindquarters, which was curing in the kitchen, wrapped in a damp cheesecloth.

He stepped outside and shaded his eyes from the sun. The rider evidently knew the way to his house because he passed by and went to the road that circled back around the York cemetery and led to the backyard. There was a road up through the field, but anyone coming that way would have to pass through two gates.

Lew's father had bought the place from the York family, and they allowed him to ride around the edge of their small cemetery in order to get to the house. The Yorks kept the cemetery groomed, using scythes and hoes at least twice a year, and there were always copperheads and cottonmouths hiding in the tall weeds whenever the Yorks rode down from Alpena to tend their graveyard.

Winter had kept the weeds down, so Lew was able to see the rider clearly as he whipped past the tombstones and headed for the house. He saw that the man was laying leather and spurs to the horse, slapping its rump with the tail ends of the reins and clapping his heels into the horse's flanks.

Lew didn't recognize either horse or rider from that distance, but he went back inside the barn, picked up his hat, and put it on. He started walking up to the gate in front of the house, passing the pond that provided fish and water for the stock. All of the snow in the field had melted during the day, and the path to the house was slightly muddy. A bass broke the water in the pond, causing a big splash. Mentally, Lew estimated the weight of the fish at about six pounds at least.

The rider spotted Lew and reined up shortly before he would have disappeared behind the house. He waved his arms frantically and Lew waved back, puzzled by the display.

"Lew Zane, come quick," he heard the rider call.

"I'm coming," Lew shouted back and increased his pace, breaking into a trot as he approached the gate. The rider dismounted and tied his horse to a hitching provided for visitors, then walked around the side of the house to the front, coming to a halt between two large box elders that provided shade in the summertime. The fence out front was home as well to some large black walnut trees, and to the side were stately oaks and hickories, their limbs still bare, bereft of leaves on this next to the last day of March in 1881.

As he approached the front gate, Lew recognized the man standing in the yard. He was the son of the Baptist preacher, Reverend Harlan Cobb's boy, Percy. Lew remembered Percy from school, when they were both boys, but he didn't know him to be so excitable. He had always seemed subdued, awkward, a mere shadow to his fire-and-brimstone-snorting father. Yet here he was, the preacher's boy, riding hell-bent for leather way out here yelling and hollering like a hysterical woman.

"Lew, you got to hurry," Percy railed, his voice rising to a squeaky pitch. "Something bad's happened in town and you got to go there real quick. Pa says so."

Lew lifted the latch on the gate and went into the yard. He had hung an old plowshare attached to a length of rope as a sash weight so that the gate would swing shut whenever it was opened and released. The gate clattered, its wooden slats loosened over time.

"Slow down, Percy," he said as the young man rushed up to him, his starchy hair sprouting from his scalp in all directions, his eyes wide as two-bit pieces, owlish with the fever of his excitement. His sharply pointed Adam's apple bobbing up and down as he spoke, it stretched the skin until it was so taut it looked as if it might pierce his flesh.

"You got to come now. Pa says. I mean it's real bad, Lew. You got to get on your horse and come on into town."

"All right. Is your pa sick? Your ma? Did something happen to them?"

"Lew, I can't say it. Don't ask me no more. Just come on, please."

There was a pleading in Percy's voice that made him sound like he was almost whining. And he was wringing his hands as if they were stained with something he could not remove.

"Unless you tell me what's going on in town that's so urgent, Percy, I'll stay right here."

"It ain't my folks, Lew. It's your'n. Now come on."

"Mine? My folks? What in hell are you talking about?"

"Lew, just come on, will you?"

Lew grabbed Percy by his shirtfront and shook him. He stared into his eyes with a rabid glare. Percy's face blanched and he swallowed, his throat rippling the sharp edge of his Adam's apple.

"Now you tell me just what's going on with my parents, Percy, damn you. Did they tell you to come and get me?"

Percy shook his head.

"Your ma and pa, Lew. They're plumb dead. Somebody killed them right there in their store. It's just an awful thing to tell you."

If there were crows calling over by the cemetery, if there was a meadowlark trilling down by the pond, if there was a mockingbird meowing like a cat back in the pecan trees, or horses neighing down in the barn, Lew didn't hear them. If there was golden sunlight on his back, he didn't feel it. If there was the smell of wet alfalfa hay left strewn in the field after mowing, he could not detect its scent. If there was a hawk flying overhead, it cast no shadow as it raked the air on silent pinions. And if he had a heart inside his chest, it was not beating.

And if there was fresh air, he was not breathing it.

Time seemed to stop for an eternity, and if the sky had been blue that day, it was now pitch black.

Lew felt as if all the life had gone out of him. His senses swam with so many emotions he could not sort them out or define them. He was a husk, a shell, a hollow man in that terrible instant when he learned his parents were dead.

Somehow Lew found his voice, thin with fear and disbelief.

"Who? Were they murdered? What happened to them?"

"I-I don't know, Lew. The sheriff's there. A whole bunch of people. My pa said to come and get you."

"Meet me down on the road," Lew said, regaining his composure and discovering his resolve. He knew he was going to learn nothing from Percy. The boy was just shy of being an idiot. That they would send a dolt like Percy out to get him must mean that there was a lot of confusion in town. He wanted to know so many things. How long they had been dead, how they had died.

As Percy left to get back on his horse, Lew ran inside the house, went to his bedroom. There, he went to the wall and slipped his pistol and holster off the wooden dowel where they hung. The gun belt was filled with .44/40 cartridges, the Colt loaded, the bluing shining with a thin patina of oil rubbed into the metal. He strapped on his pistol and ran out of the house. He slipped open the gate and ran to the barn, his heart pumping at an accelerated pace, his mind filled with anticipation and dread.

Inside the barn, Lew went to the tack room, opened the door, and quickly went inside. He grabbed his saddle, blanket, and reins and dashed to the stall where Ruben, the big red roan gelding, was still chomping on grain and hay. He opened the stall and went inside. He slipped the bridle over Ruben's head, fastened the chin strap, made sure the single bit was comfortably inside Ruben's mouth. He threw the blanket over Ruben's back, and then the saddle. The horse lifted its head, still chewing the last of the grain in its mouth, the bit clattering against its teeth.

He led Ruben out of the stall and out into the lot, where he mounted the horse. He saw Percy waiting just beyond the gate, looking at that distance like an ungainly undertaker in his dark shirt and trousers. Lew rode to the gate, slipped the wire from the top post, and lifted the latch. The gate swung open and he rode through it, then turned Ruben and pulled the gate back into place until the latch clicked tight.

"Let's go," Lew said, and clapped his heels into Ruben's flanks. Just a touch was all it took. Ruben broke into a trot, then after another gentle kick, gamboled into a gallop. In moments, Lew had left Percy behind, swallowing Ruben's dust. Lew pushed his hat down more tightly on his head and let Ruben run. It was three miles to his parents' store and those miles could not pass fast enough for Lew.

Shadows striped the tree-lined road and puddled up in the ditches. The wind whipped at Lew's face, cooling the sweat that dripped from under his hat brim and eyebrows, streaked down his neck in salty rivulets.

He reached the Alpena-Huntsville road and turned left toward his folks' store. He saw their mule and buggy and a crowd of townspeople lining the banks of the little creek, the townspeople craning their necks as other men held them back. There were horses tied to the hitch rail out front, and he headed that way. He glanced over his shoulder and saw Percy just turning onto the main road, a scarecrow jouncing in the saddle like a sack of turnips.

Lew wrapped his reins around the hitch rail and walked up to the porch. A man stepped out to bar his way, then recognized Lew.

"Zane, you'd better brace yourself, son. There's a sight inside that's as brutal as it gets."

Lew looked at the man's face until recognition arose in his mind's memory, like a creek-bottom fog parting in a gentle zephyr. It was the foreman at the stave factory, a burly slope-shouldered man named Sam Huff. He now sported a tin badge on his shirt, and Lew figured that Sheriff Don Swanson had deputized him.

"My folks," Lew said. "Are they dead?"

"Son, it's not a pretty sight, but Don's in there and we've got witnesses, I think."

"Can I go in?"

"You sure you want to? Nothing's been cleaned up. I mean . . ."

"I know what you mean, Sam. Step aside."

The foreman was not used to taking orders from young whippersnappers, but he stood to one side and let Lew pass through the door.

Sheriff Swanson looked up as Lew came in, notified by the jangling bell that bounced up and down on a metal strap like some demented jack-in-the-box with a clapper in its stomach.

"Lew, it's real bad," Swanson said.

Lew recognized the doctor squatted down next to something that didn't look human. His assistant was kneeling over another shapeless mass of blood and clothes. Lew's stomach swirled with a cloud of winged insects, and he felt the acid sting of bile threaten to claw its way up his throat. A feeling of being smothered came over him and his legs turned to rubber, his knees to jelly.

Dr. Ted Rankins must have sensed Lew's presence, for he turned and looked up, concern in his eyes. A stethoscope dangled from his neck and his fingertips were red with blood. His shaven head gleamed with sweat, its smoothness marred by blue veins that bubbled like boiling worms just beneath his scalp.

"Lew, I'm real sorry," Rankins said and stood up, as if to offer comfort if needed.

That's when Lew saw the mangled, distorted features of his father, his head lying in a dark pool of dried blood, the flies already clustering over the mess like miniature buzzards.

And the floor dropped a foot beneath Lew and turned to rubber. He felt himself falling while the sun streamed through the windows and dust danced luridly in its beams, while the silence rose up in the room like some enormous smothering, invisible cloud that reeked of desolation and death.

6

THE SHERIFF PUT OUT AN ARM TO BRACE LEW, KEEP HIM
from falling. From across the room, Reverend Cobb rushed
over and grabbed Lew by the shoulders.

"Such a shock," Cobb said.

"I'm all right," Lew said, pushing Sheriff Swanson's
arm away from his chest. But the room still swam around
him and his legs still felt as if they were made of rubber.

"You're still just a mite giddy, Lew," Cobb said, squeezing his fingers so that they tightened on Lew's shoulders.
"We can walk outside, if you wish. We could, perhaps, talk
about this."

"No," Lew said. "I want to see it. I want to see it all."

He shook himself away from the preacher and shoved
Swanson aside.

That's when Lew saw his mother. His father was all
crumpled up, looked shriveled and small, unlike he ever
did in real life. But his mother was lying splayed out, one
arm slightly raised, rigid, a leg lying crooked beneath her,
stiff as a board, her bonnet askew on her bloody head. She
looked, at first glance, like an oversized rag doll with its

eyes closed and spatters of blood on her cheeks that could be mistaken for freckles.

Lew recoiled in horror at the sight of his once-vibrant mother. Lying there on the floor like something tossed in a scrap heap. He sucked in a breath at the shock of it, then let it out in a long, slow sigh that was almost a sob.

"You shouldn't have to see this, son," Swanson said. "And I see you're packing iron. You better slip off that gun belt and let me have it."

Lew shook himself away from an onrush of grief and self-pity that threatened to overwhelm and drown him in a sea of sorrow. He looked Swanson straight in the eye, his jaw tightening.

"I heard you've got witnesses," Lew said. "Do you know who did this, Don?"

"Well, now, hold your horses, Lew. We're still working on that. There's nothing official yet."

"I'm not giving you my gun, Don. And don't you ask me again."

"For your own protection, Lew, I think you ought to give me that gun belt till you've had a chance to cool down some."

"I'm not going to disarm myself, Don. If the man who murdered my parents is arrested and brought to trial, I'll let justice serve its course. Good enough?"

"I reckon," Swanson said.

Lew turned to Rankins.

"Doc, how were my folks killed?"

"They were beaten to death, Lew."

"With what?"

"I don't know for sure, but just looking at the wounds, it looks like they were pistol-whipped."

"What about this witness, Don? What does he say?"

"There were several folks who heard the commotion down here and saw two boys running from the back of the store. They had their horses tied down in the creek bottom, upstream a ways."

"Do these witnesses know who these boys were?" Lew asked.

Swanson shook his head. "I'm not going to tell you what's only a rumor right now, Lew. There's a lot to sort out and we haven't even started."

"Who's we?"

"Me and my deputy, the doc here, anybody who can help us."

"Why did they murder my folks?"

"Well, we found a strongbox. I reckon the motive was robbery."

Lew snorted in derision.

"What?" Swanson said.

"They never kept much money in that strongbox," Lew said. "Never enough to tempt a serious thief."

"Well, the strongbox was broke open and we found it back in the storeroom lying on the floor. Damned kids," Swanson said.

"Kids?" Lew's eyebrows arched and his eyes widened.

"Young fellers," Swanson said.

"They from around here?" Lew asked.

"I can't say," Swanson said.

"You mean you won't say."

"Six of one, half a dozen of the other."

"Are you going to arrest those killers?" Lew asked point-blank.

Swanson seemed to squirm inside his clothes. He didn't answer right away.

"Lew," Dr. Rankins said, his voice low, just above a whisper, "do you want to . . . I mean, I'm going to cover your folks up . . . do you want to . . . ?"

Lew knew what Dr. Rankins meant.

"No, Doc," he said. "I want to remember them as they were. I'll say my good-byes later." And in my own way, he thought.

The doctor took two sheets from his assistant and

spread them over the corpses. Then he stood up. He put a hand on Lew's shoulder.

"I'm sorry, Lew," Rankins said.

"I am too, Doc." Lew turned back to the sheriff. "I'm still waiting to hear what you're going to do, Don."

"Well, not much I can do right now. We have one witness, so called, but I don't know if he's reliable or not. And there are other considerations."

"Who's the witness?" Lew asked. "Who saw these boys murder my folks?"

"I don't think you need to know that right now, Lew."

"I damned sure do, Don. Either you tell me or I'll walk outside and start asking questions."

The sheriff shifted his feet and sucked in a breath. He let the air out through his nose, shook his head.

"Damn it, Lew. You've got to get off my back about this. I'm still sorting through this mess."

"This mess? My folks have been murdered. Brutally murdered. And you know who did it. But you won't tell me. They might be nothing to you, but they were my life. I deserve to know who killed them. I need to know. Now. Right now, Don."

"I ain't going to tell you now, Lew. You'll just have to wait until I finish investigatin'."

Two men came through the back door, passed through the storeroom, carrying litters that appeared to be left over from the Civil War. They stood there, looking at the sheet-draped bodies.

Lew didn't recognize either man.

"Take the remains to Doc Rankins's office," Sheriff Swanson said to them.

The doctor looked at Lew.

"I'll examine them and bathe them, Lew," Rankins said. "Tomorrow, your folks will be transported to the undertaker's in Alpena. Goodwin's. You can see them there, or ride up with the wagon."

"Thanks, Doc," Lew said. He balled his fists up, trying to squeeze back the tears that seeped through his blinking eyelids. There was something so cold and final about the removal of the bodies. He wanted to clear the room and kneel down next to his mother and hold her dead hand in his and say something to her, even though he knew she could no longer hear him. He wanted to take her into his arms and hold her lifeless body and let the tears flow until his grief was drained from his aching heart.

And he wanted to touch his father's torn and ravaged face and smooth the lumps and wipe away the bruises and wash away the blood that caked his skin like ugly scabs.

But he was frozen in place, numb with an overwhelming grief, a sadness that was so deep it was almost beyond comprehension. He wanted to do these things, but there were so many people there, all gawking at him, so that he could not bring himself to perform such private acts in public.

"I'll ride with them up to Alpena," Lew said to the doctor.

Lew watched as the two men put his mother's body on one of the stretchers. They carried it out back, then returned after a few minutes to do the same with his father's corpse. The deputy, poking around in the pantry, emerged with a slip of paper in his hand. He handed it to Swanson.

"Found that on the floor in the pantry," he said. "It must have fallen out of that strongbox. I can see the outline in the dust where they kept the box."

Lew said nothing, but studied the sheriff as he read what was written on the piece of paper.

The sheriff looked up at Lew.

"I know what that is," Lew said. "My mother kept track of everything. If that was in the strongbox, it will say how much money they had in there."

"I wasn't going to tell you, Lew," Swanson said. "Thought it might be too painful right now."

"I know they didn't keep much money here at the store."

"No, I reckon not."

"So, how much did those two murdering bastards steal?" Lew asked, trying to control his rage.

"Forty dollars is what it says here on this piece of paper."

"Forty dollars," Lew repeated, as if he was in a daze. "For forty pieces of silver, those bastards murdered two fine people. Twenty dollars apiece. Life's cheap around here, I reckon." The bitterness in Lew's tone of voice was not lost on those still in the room. They all looked down sheepishly at their boots, the floor, the blood spattered all over.

"It's a crying shame," Swanson said, sucking in a breath.

Lew started to walk toward the back door.

"Where you going?" Swanson asked.

"I'm going to see where they tied their horses, take a look at those tracks."

"You aren't going to do something foolish, are you now?"

Lew stopped and turned back to face the sheriff, a dangerous glare in his eyes.

"Don, are you just going to stand there and let those boys go out and spend that money, maybe get drunk and joke about what they done?"

"I'm still going over the evidence, Lew. I told you that."

"You know who did it. You've got a rope. There are plenty of trees around here."

"Now we don't do things like that no more, Lew. If those boys are guilty, I'll arrest them and they'll go up in front of a judge and he'll say what's to be done."

"I know what has to be done, Don."

"If you break the law, Lew, I'll have to come after you. Same as any criminal."

Lew fixed the sheriff with a look of contempt and stalked out through the storeroom. Outside, he saw a crowd of people lining the creek, watching the cart haul his parents into Osage, to the doctor's office. They turned and looked at him, some with pity, some with curiosity, like people waiting for a parade to start and wondering if Lew was part of it. He could hear their whispers as he walked past them and up the creek. He stared at the ground, looking for tracks. He saw that people had walked all over the place and none of the footprints stood out.

He found where the two killers had tied up their horses. The ground was not so disturbed there, but he saw the sheriff's boot marks and what he took to be the boot marks of the two who had robbed his folks and murdered them. He squatted down to study them more carefully.

He studied every scuff mark on the soles, every nick, every anomaly that made them distinctive.

He would remember those tracks.

Just then a man walked up to him, away from the crowd out back of the store.

"Lew, I seen them jaspers what butchered your folks," the man said.

Lew recognized him as Cletus Sisco, a man more often drunk than not, and perhaps a little addled as well.

"Are you the eyewitness Don Swanson told me about?"

Sisco grinned. There were gaps in his upper row of teeth and not many left on the bottom.

"Yeah, I am. I seen 'em real good, Lew."

Out of the corner of his eye, Lew saw Swanson step out onto the back porch and then look at him. Don began heading his way, walking fast.

"Tell me their names, Cletus," Lew said.

Sisco hesitated as Swanson drew closer.

"Lew, you get away from that witness," Swanson called.

Sisco's eyes rolled wildly in their sockets.

Lew wondered if he was going to have to choke those names out of him before Swanson interfered any more than he already had.

And then he wondered if he was going to have to draw his pistol and throw down on Sheriff Swanson.

Hours went by in the space of a few seconds, and Sisco wasn't talking and Swanson was already less than fifty paces away from spoiling everything.

7

SWANSON YELLED AT CLETUS SISCO NEXT.

"Cletus, you get the hell out of here right now. Don't you be talkin' to that man."

Lew stepped in close to Sisco.

"Tell me their names, Cletus. Now. Or I'll blow you all to hell where you stand."

Cletus gulped, swallowing air, but he blurted out the names.

"It were that Pope boy, Wiley, I seen, and Canby, the one they call Fritzie. Fritz, I think."

"You done real good, Cletus," Lew whispered as Sheriff Swanson came up behind Sisco, grabbed him by the arm, and whirled him around. Swanson's face was livid with anger. The corded veins on his neck swelled up blue against the skin.

"I'll lock you up, Cletus, if you go shootin' off your damned mouth. You won't be worth a damn as a witness if you go yapping to every Tom, Dick, and Harry what you know, or think you know. You hear me, Cletus?"

"Yes, sir, Mr. Swanson, I hear you real good. I won't say nothin' to nobody, no siree, sir."

"Seems to me, Don, you're overstepping your authority a bit," Lew said. "Man's got a right to speak his piece. That's in the U.S. Constitution."

"Not in Carroll County he don't," Swanson said. "And not in Osage, Arkansas, neither. Not as long as I'm sheriff. Now, Cletus, you get on out of here and mind what I told you."

"Yes, sir, Mr. Swanson. I'm done gone," Cletus said, and he shuffled off through the ragged snow and the fallen leaves, leaving a swath along the creek where there was still some shade along the banks.

Swanson looked Lew up and down. He was still fuming, but seemed reluctant to get down off his soapbox. Lew could tell that he liked being in charge. There was little enough for a sheriff to do in Osage, and Swanson had been elected mainly because nobody else wanted the job. The job, Lew knew, consisted mostly of overseeing elections in the basement of the Baptist church, seeing to it that there was no electioneering going on within so many feet of the church, or leading folks inside and telling them who to cast their votes for, which was illegal. The rest of the time Swanson spent pitching horseshoes and chewing tobacco while sipping tea the ladies provided for the voters and the election workers. When not working the elections, Swanson spent his days whittling or riding around to the farms where he knew the women baked pies, and standing around taking up people's time so long they had to feed him to get rid of him.

There had been no murders in Osage since Lew and his family had lived there, and he doubted if Swanson knew a clue from a horse apple.

"You better get on to home too, Lew," Swanson said. "You can't do no good here and I've got investigating to do."

"Shouldn't you be getting up a posse and going after Wiley Pope and Fritz Canby about now, Don?"

Swanson's face seemed to go through all the variations

of the color red, starting with a pale pink, suffusing to a rose, and ending up in deep purple.

"Now where in hell did you get them names, Lew? That damned Cletus. I ought to nail his hide to the barn door and set the barn afire, I declare. The man don't know to keep his damned mouth shut."

"Hell, Don, by now everybody in Osage probably knows who killed my folks, and by nightfall everybody in Carroll County will know it. Now, are you going after those two boys and put 'em in jail or not?"

Swanson pulled a plug of tobacco from his pocket and bit off a corner. He tongued the fragment to one side of his mouth and started worrying it with his teeth. He put the plug back in his pocket and let out a deep sigh.

"Tomorrow, Lew, if I get everything done today I got to get done, I'll ride over to the county seat in Berryville and give my report to the county prosecutor. It will be up to him to issue the warrants. Then, if he does that, I reckon Sheriff Billy Jim Colfax up in Alpena will have to serve those warrants."

Lew snorted. "All that's going to take time, while Wiley and Fritz go free. You ought to go after them now and lock them up in the Alpena jail. Then go to Berryville."

"You think I can just go up to Alpena and arrest Wiley Pope? Hell, Billy Jim would probably throw me in jail."

"Why?" Lew asked.

"Well, for one thing, Wiley's pa is Virgil Pope and more than half of Osage and nearly all of Alpena work for the man."

"You don't work for him. And neither do I, Don."

"Looky, this here town's dependent on making barrel staves. Virgil owns the lumber company what delivers the wood. And matter of fact, old Virgil owns the factory here."

"I didn't know that."

"It ain't common knowledge." Swanson spat a stream of tobacco juice out of the side of his mouth. It splattered on wet rock like a squashed bug.

"That doesn't make Virgil Pope or his son above the law," Lew said.

"Some would say, and I ain't sayin' who, mind you, would say Virgil *is* the law."

"Not in my book, he isn't."

"Maybe you've got the wrong book," Swanson said. "Look, I got a lot to do. I got to set guards to watch over the store today and tonight. I'll be off to Berryville tomorrow likely, and you better go on home and tend to the stock."

"I'm going to clean the store and fix that back door," Lew said.

"Suit yourself. Just don't go off and do anything half-cocked. Let the law handle this."

"Sure," Lew said, but he said it only to get Swanson off his back. All he could think about was that those two killers were running free and the law wasn't doing a damned thing about it. He walked back to the store with Swanson, who dispersed the crowd and assigned someone to watch over the store until the back door was fixed.

"You want somebody to take your folks' buggy back home, Lew?" Swanson asked.

"Naw, I'll do it," Lew said, hoping the sheriff would go back to town and leave him alone.

"You need help cleaning up?"

"Nope."

"All right," Swanson said.

Lew went inside the store, which was empty. He could feel his parents, feel their presence, even though he knew they were dead and would never come there again. A great sadness overwhelmed him when he walked to the place where they had died. He cringed to think of their final moments, the brutality of their murders. There was blood all over the floor, and he considered leaving it there as a reminder to all who came there of what had happened.

He walked back to the storeroom and found a mop and bucket, a bar of lye soap. He walked out to the creek and filled the bucket, came back inside. He set to scrubbing the floor, dipping the bar of lye soap in the bucket and sloshing it so that it made some suds. He poured the sudsy mixture on the floor and began to scrub with the mop.

He didn't hear her enter, but sniffed a faint perfume that made him turn around.

"I thought you might need some help," she said.

It was Seneca Jones, a girl he had known in school. She still wore long pigtails, the ends tied with little blue ribbons. Her black hair shone like a crow's sun-splashed wing and she smelled of lilacs and honeysuckle. Her blue eyes crackled light, but there were shadows of sorrow and concern in them too.

"Seneca," he said, feeling a little awkward. He had not seen her since school, although he had thought about her from time to time. He was sure she was sweet on a feller he didn't like much, a boy named Tommy Burrell. "What are you doing here? It's not a good place for you to be."

"Lew, I'm real sorry about your folks. I came here to help you clean up. If you want to fix that back door, I'll finish up in here. You're doing it all wrong anyway."

"Huh?"

"Let me do it," she said.

She pushed him aside, got down on her hands and knees. She had a scrub brush in her hand, and she dipped it into the bucket and then began to scrub the floor. Her gingham dress flowed over the backs of her legs, but he could see her ankles. They were slim and graceful like the legs of a thoroughbred racing horse.

"I'll fix the back door," he said.

"Good. Then my daddy won't have to guard the store tonight. Sheriff Swanson assigned him to do that before he left."

Lew walked outside and saw Seneca's father standing there, a double-barreled shotgun cradled in his arms.

"Ed," Lew said.

"Howdy, Lew. Going to fix that door, are you?"

"Yeah. I'll put on a new latch. I know where my . . . where my pa keeps a supply."

"Took a rock to it, looks like," Ed Jones said. "Smashed it all to hell."

Lew gritted his teeth. The last thing he wanted just then was a lot of small talk. Especially from Seneca's father. All Lew could think of was her inside on her hands and knees, working like a scrubwoman.

"You can go on home, Ed," Lew said. "Store will be locked up when I finish."

"Nope. Can't do that. Swannie told me to stand guard here until he comes and gets me. And that's just what I'm going to do."

"All right. There's no need, though."

Lew went back inside and rummaged in the storeroom for the tools and the fixtures he needed. The place reeked of whiskey, and he saw that the bottles on the shelf had been disturbed. So the boys had gotten into the liquor and gotten drunked up before they murdered his mother and father. He wanted to strangle them with his bare hands.

The door was not damaged and Lew fixed it in jig time, found a padlock that would fit inside. When he walked into the store, Seneca was drying the floor with the mop. He could still see the stains from the blood, but they were faint and, in time, would fade into the wood and be hardly noticeable.

"Thanks, Seneca. I appreciate your help."

"What are you going to do now, Lew?" she asked. "I mean with your life."

"I can't think about my life right now," he said.

She set the mop down, leaning it against the bucket. She walked over to him, looked into his eyes. Hers were such a deep clear blue, they almost looked as if they were painted. They were beautiful eyes. And hypnotic. He remembered looking into them when he first saw her and how dizzy he had gotten, which shamed him back then. He was only eleven or twelve, but he was smitten. He turned away from her.

"You can't run from your feelings," she said.

"I'm not running."

"They'll catch up to you. Tonight. When you're alone. At odd times."

"I reckon."

"I know," she said.

And then he remembered that her mother had died a couple of years before. He and his parents had gone to Gena's funeral. It was sad and Seneca had cried when the casket was lowered into the grave. He had wanted to go to her then and put his arms around her and comfort her, but that damned Burrell boy was with her.

"Yes," he said, "I reckon you do. When your ma died, I wanted to come over after . . . afterwards, but you were with Tommy."

"I broke off with Tommy after that. He just wanted to take advantage of me."

"Sorry."

She reached out and touched his arm.

"Lew, if you ever want to talk, or need to talk, you come on by, hear?"

"Thanks, Seneca. I might stop by sometime."

"And don't do anything foolish."

"What do you mean?"

"One thing I know," she said. "When someone you love very much dies, you get angry. You get angry at anybody and anything. You even get angry with God. I did."

"I'm not angry with God. He didn't have anything to do with this."

"No, but those two boys did. You've got to let the law take care of their punishment."

He wanted to say, "What law?" but he didn't. He just felt the heat from Seneca's hand and how it streamed through his arm and into his body and mind. For a moment or two, he wasn't thinking about Wiley and Fritz. He was looking into Seneca's eyes and getting that same giddy feeling as he'd had when he first met her.

The real world seemed to melt away and the tragedy that had happened grow dim. At that moment, he lost the power of speech, along with most of his senses, and he didn't want Seneca to leave and there was no place he wanted to go without her.

8

THE SADNESS CAME TO LEW AGAIN AS HE WAS DRIVING THE
buggy home. He had gathered provisions from the store,
loaded them in the buggy, tied his horse to the rear, then
locked up. Seneca had gone home and, finally, Swanson
came to tell her father, Ed, to go on home as well after
Swanson inspected the premises and decided the store was
as secure as it was going to be. The sheriff seemed satisfied
that Lew was going to take the mule and buggy home and
leave justice to the law. Lew didn't tell Swanson that, as far
as he was concerned, he was on a very short rope.

The long shadows of afternoon striped the road back to
the farm. Lew could feel his folks sitting beside him in the
buggy, his mother on his left, his father on the right. He
could smell them. He could almost feel them. There was a
sadness to the shadows and a sadness to the trees that lined
the road. There was a sadness in the failing sunlight, a sadness to the end of a long sad day.

Most of the snow had melted and there was mud on the
road. But the mule, Old Pete, plodded right along unmind-
ful of the cold and the wet. Ruben trotted along behind,

fighting every step in a puddle or a mud-slicked spot, ranging from right to left to avoid splattering his hocks.

And the sadness grew in Lew's heart as he approached the lane to the front pasture. He would unhitch the buggy and put Pete up, feed him, but then he'd have to ride Ruben over to Twyman's place, another two or three miles down the road and at the very end of the road. Twyman and his wife were regular hands his father used as part-time help, but Lew was going to need him to tend to the stock, and he would ask Twyman's wife, Edna, to mind the store for a time. Twyman Butterfield was a good worker. His small farm didn't take up all his time, and earned him little or no money, so Lew's father hired him to work four or five days a week in the spring and summer, and only two or three days in the winter.

Lew set the brake on the buggy after he reached the front gate. He stepped down and slipped the wire over the post, swung the gate wide, then returned to the buggy, got in, and drove it through. He left the gate open and drove the buggy up to the back of the barn. He ran the buggy inside, unhitched Pete, and put him in a stall. He poured a hatful of grain in the bin and then stored the buggy. Ruben was stamping his feet and snorting by the time Lew led him back outside and climbed into the saddle. The sun had just set and the valley seemed cast in a gray atmosphere of doom, as if he had stepped into a crypt, with the hills for walls and the sky for a ceiling.

Lew could hardly look at the house. It was dark amid the leafless trees that surrounded it, and looked so forlorn and empty when he glanced up as he rounded the front of the barn. He should have ridden up and lighted a lamp, but he wanted to make sure Twyman came to his place at first light and got Edna to the store in time to open for business the next day.

He closed the front gate after he rode out onto the road. The road ran west toward the scars of the sunset still marring the sky, with just a glimmer of light marking the horizon beyond the trees. He passed the lane that led up past the York cemetery and to his house, passed by a bend in Osage Creek, and then on, between sloping hills where blackberry brambles provided cover for rabbits and quail, as well as for a host of lesser creatures.

Near the road's end, he turned north onto the lane that led to the Butterfield property. By then it was full dark, and stars sprinkled the sky with silver fireflies that winked across the vast distance of space.

He saw the lamp glow in the windows of Twyman's house, and heard a horse whicker from the stables beyond the house. Ruben picked up his gait and trotted up to the hitch rail in front of the little picket fence that surrounded the house and yard.

"Hello the house," Lew called. The front door opened, spilling a slash of honeyed light onto the porch.

"Lew, is that you?" Twyman called, holding a flat hand above his bushy eyebrows as he peered out into the darkness.

"Good evening," Lew said, and reined up Ruben, then swung out of the saddle. He wrapped the reins around the hitch rail and walked to the gate.

"You're out late, Lew. Come on in. Edny's about to set supper."

"Be right there, Twyman. Go on and eat. I can't stay."

As Lew passed through the gate and into the yard, a dog slunk out from under the porch, wagging its tail. When Lew patted its head, it wagged its entire body.

"Hello, Sandman," Lew said, and the dog wagged its tail so hard, and its body, it nearly doubled up on itself. Thin and rangy, the dog was dark brown. Its ribs stood out like barrel slats and there were pieces of hide missing from the mange.

"Sandman, you go on back under the porch," Twyman said as Lew mounted the steps. Inside, Lew smelled the food as Edna emerged from the kitchen, a towel around her waist, her graying hair pulled back away from her face and tied in the back with a faded ribbon.

"What brings you out so late, Lew?" Edna said, smiling, her teeth dark pegs in her mouth, stained brown and black from years of chewing on some unknown substance.

Lew took off his hat when she entered the room. He held it by the brim in both hands.

It was obvious to Lew that the Butterfields did not know what had happened in town that day. He hated to be the one to break the news to them.

"I got to ask you both a big favor," Lew said as Edna waved him to the lumpy divan.

"Set down, Lew," she said. "Supper'll be on the table in just a minute. Lord, I've got enough to feed an army."

"You got your pistol on," Twyman said to Lew. "You been huntin'?"

Lew shook his head. He did not sit on the divan, but stood there, groping for the words he knew he had to say.

"Maybe you both better sit down, Twy," Lew said.

Edna picked up on the change in Lew's tone. Twyman just stood there, a bewildered look on his face.

"What's wrong, Lew?" she asked. "You look like you swallowed poison."

Lew drew in a breath, then let it out through his nostrils in a whoosh of air. His eyes began to turn moist with welling tears.

"Ma and Pa were killed this morning," he said, a rasp in his voice that had not been there before. "Down at the store."

Edna's face seemed to collapse as the muscles gave way to shock. Twyman stood there, the color on his face turning to paste.

"Killed?" Edna said, the word coming out in a soft gasp.

Lew nodded, blinking at the tears blurring his vision.

Edna walked to the divan and sank down. Twyman stood there, as if struck dumb, his expression blank.

"Oh, dear," Edna said. "Oh, dear."

"What happened?" Twyman said, his voice a dull monotone, flat, lifeless.

"Two boys from Alpena broke into the store and beat my folks to death," Lew said. "Robbed them."

"Who?" Edna asked.

"Wiley Pope and Fritz Canby." Lew wiped his eyes and breathed deep to calm himself. "I'm going to be busy for a few days. I'd like you to watch after our place, Twyman. Edna, if you could open the store in case folks drop by. I've got the key here." He reached into this pocket and held out a set of keys to Edna. She took them.

"Of course," she said. "Twy and I will want to come to the funeral. Oh, dear, I just can't imagine. . . ."

"It don't seem possible," Twyman said. "I mean, they was both so alive and all. Lew, I'm real sorry. Edna and I both are."

"Thanks, Twy. You look after things, will you? I have to ride up to the undertaker's with my folks and see the sheriff up in Alpena tomorrow. I'll pay you both when I get back."

"Lordy, don't you fret about that," Edna said. "Now, come and have some supper with us, Lew."

"No, I've got a lot to do. Thanks. But that reminds me, Twy. I shot a buck this morning. There's fresh meat in the springhouse. You bring home what you need tomorrow night."

"You kill that big ten-point buck?" Twyman asked.

"Yeah," Lew said, and somehow it seemed wrong that he had taken the buck's life. He had never felt that way before, but he felt that way now. Life seemed mighty precious just then.

He had started for the door when Twyman came to life and reached out, grabbed Lew's arm.

"You want some company over to your place tonight?" Twyman asked.

Lew shook his head. He had to get out of there. He was suffocating with the grief that was building in the room. He didn't want sympathy just then. He needed to clear his own head and break the pull the Butterfields had on him.

"Good night, Lew," Twyman said.

"Good night."

Edna didn't say anything until Lew reached the door.

"Lew," she said, "isn't this your birthday? Seems to me your ma . . ."

Lew turned. He felt himself choking up.

"Yeah," he said. "Ma was going to bake a cake for to-night. I have to go. G'night, Edna, Twy."

. And then Lew was out the door before either could say anything more to him. He felt as if he had escaped from a prison.

The night air splashed cool against his face as he ran to the gate, opened it, and went out of the yard. The dog came wagging out to the gate and stood there, its entire body twisting back and forth just like its tail. Lew mounted Ruben and turned the horse into the lane. He looked back once to see Twyman standing framed in the doorway, the light from the lamps in the front room spraying around his dark silhouette like a golden mist. He heard Twyman call to his dog, ordering it back under the front porch.

Now that he had left the Butterfields', Lew dreaded going home to his empty house. Some birthday, he thought. He was now an orphan. That was a hell of a birthday present.

He shook off those thoughts, and sniffed the cool air of evening. The sun had set and the night seemed a comfort to him. Darkness hid so many things, his grief among them. No one could see his red eyes or the streaks of tears on his face. But he knew he must not wallow in self-pity. The But-terfields had had their share of tragedies in life. They had no children now, but Edna had given birth to three, two daughters and a son. All had died, from sickness or from accidents. Yet they went on, living their simple lives, eking out an existence on a hardscrabble farm, not wanting much, not asking much.

There was no reason he could not do the same, he thought. But it was mighty hard. God, it was hard, riding home to a place of emptiness, his folks dead, his life full of holes where they had been. It was a godawful feeling, all right, but if he kept himself busy, if he did something to avenge their deaths, then he would not take the grieving so hard.

But what could he do? Sheriff Swanson had said the law would take care of the two boys who had murdered his parents. Could he trust the law? Swanson wasn't a real sheriff. He was just a town sheriff the people had voted in because they wanted to sleep nights and not worry. But Swanson had not protected his parents, or anyone else. He was just a man with a badge and he was standing around waiting for someone else to do his job. He wouldn't arrest anyone, let alone those two murdering boys.

When Lew reached the house, his grief had been replaced by a burning anger, and as he dismounted and stormed toward the back door, he let out a yell.

"Well, by God, somebody better arrest those murdering bastards."

Ruben whickered as the echoes of Lew's shout died away in the hollows and hills. By the time Lew entered the house, he was weeping again, unashamedly, sobbing aloud in the empty chamber of the house that seemed then like a tomb, with him, buried alive in it, as helpless as Swanson to get justice or bring his parents back to life.

9

LEW FELL INTO BED THAT BIRTHDAY NIGHT WITHOUT EATING supper. He slept fitfully, rising often to walk through the empty house in a trance. He went into his parents' bedroom several times, smelled the flowery scent of his mother, the masculine musk of his father, until he was nearly smothered with their absence, their lingering presence. Like a sleepwalker, he roamed the rooms as if expecting his mother or his father to appear out of the shadows and put their arms around him. He was all wept out, suddenly devoid of all feelings because the ones he'd had were so tangled and bewildering. He remained in a stupor until he heard the cock crow and the whippoorwill go silent just before dawn.

As Lew bathed and dressed, he still felt as if he was walking through mud or quicksand. His movements were slow, lethargic, and he thought that he felt that way because he lacked sleep. But it was more than that. He was still in a state of shock not only over the murder of his parents, but over the brutality and senselessness of it. The boys had come to rob his folks. They didn't have to kill them. Although, when he thought real hard about it, the boys might have had the notion that the Zanes had money hidden in the store. Even he had heard such rumors. Perhaps those boys had believed the stories, even though everyone in Osage knew the tales were not true.

Twyman came as Lew was tightening the single cinch on Ruben's saddle. He was dressed, as usual, in faded overalls, wore an old deerstalker cap and lace-up work boots. His caterpillar eyebrows were bushier than usual, plumped up, Lew supposed, by the morning dew and creek fog. He knew Twyman had walked the three miles from his place, the distance probably shortened because Twyman always walked through the woods and not on the road.

"Anything particular you want me to look after, Lew?"

"No, just see that the stock is fed and watered. Don't forget that deer meat in the springhouse."

"Did you eat supper last night?"

"I nibbled some," Lew lied. "I wasn't very hungry."

"I'll take Edna in to the store by and by, then come on back here."

"Fine. I appreciate it. Take the buggy if you want, Twy."

Lew rode straight to the doctor's office, knowing it was still early. But there were people about and the stave factory was alive with the sounds of saws and machinery. Harlan Cobb and his son, Percy, were opening the doors of the church. Lew cringed. They'd probably want to hold some kind of service for his folks and he had strong feelings about that, which he probably wouldn't voice aloud because it might hurt Reverend Cobb's feelings.

Lew tied Ruben up at the hitch ring set in a concrete block outside Dr. Rankins's home, which also served as his office. He knocked on the door and heard footsteps. Always a good sign, he thought, that someone was up and about.

The door opened and Lew reared back in surprise.

"Good morning, Lew," Seneca said almost cheerily. "Come on in."

"What are you doing here?" he asked. Her face was fresh-scrubbed and she wore no rouge. Her pigtails hung over her shoulders, silken sculptures burnished to a high ebony sheen, contrasting sharply with the white-topped blue smock she wore over her calico dress. Her eyes sparkled like blue sapphires. He could see a shining star in each of them, mirages spun by the morning light that caught them just so.

"I came in this morning early to dress your folks and comb your mother's hair."

Lew stepped inside and into the parlor, where Seneca made him take a chair. There was a potbellied stove blazing in one corner of the room, a stack of split wood sitting in a tin basket a few feet away. The room was warm, but not hot. Lew saw that the damper was only slightly open in the tin chimney.

"I think Dr. Rankins wants to talk to you before you go in. I'll tell him you're here."

"Do they . . ."

"We did the best we could, Lew. Don't worry. Mr. Goodwin up at the undertaker's will do what's necessary to make your folks look natural."

"There's nothing natural about a dead person, Seneca."

"I know. I mean . . ."

"I know what you mean," he said. "My folks were beaten savagely. There's no fixing that with paint and glue and whatnot. I'll see them now, if you please."

"I'll go tell Dr. Rankins," she said. She didn't say it curtly, but he knew he had been short with her. He didn't mean to be. Things just boiled over inside him, and he was never one to mind his tongue when he had something on his mind. Seneca was trying to be kind. She was trying to prepare him for the grisly sight of his parents. But Dr. Rankins was not an undertaker. Seneca could comb their hair and dab on some rouge or vermilion maybe, but she couldn't fix what had been damaged.

He heard rustling in the back of the house, voices,

clinking noises. He could not imagine what Doc Rankins and Seneca were saying to each other. She was probably telling the doctor that the man in his parlor was in a nasty temper. But he wasn't. He was just nervous. It grew quiet, and Lew looked around the small room, at the benches and chairs, the little tables. There was an old Harrison newspaper on one of the tables, and on another some magazines. He read the title of one, *Harper's Weekly*. There were some dime magazines with lurid covers, the pages curled up from constant handling with sweaty hands. There was a cushion on the lone divan, and some doilies on the backs of stuffed chairs. The room smelled musty, but someone had dusted the furniture recently.

He heard the squeak of a door, and footsteps. He expected Seneca to enter the room, but it was Dr. Rankins.

"Lew, good morning."

"Good morning, Doctor."

"Before you go back there, I want to try and prepare you for what you'll see, what I found when I examined your parents last night and this morning."

"I know they won't look good, Doc."

Rankins put a hand on Lew's shoulder, as if to comfort him while he told him what he had to say.

"The beating was very brutal, Lew. It would take an expert undertaker to reconstruct their faces, especially your father's. Whoever did this had a lot of hatred inside him. I think they were both beaten with a pistol. The indentations on your father's face look like depressions made by a pistol barrel. He was struck with great force. And there is an indentation in his skull that looks as if the killer came down hard with the butt of his pistol."

Lew's jaw tightened as he bunched up his lips and squeezed back the tears.

"Go on," Lew said.

"Son, if you want to remember your folks as they were when they were alive, you won't look at what I've got in the back room. I have sheets over them now. You can take my word for it that these were your folks. It might be better that way."

Lew shifted the weight on his boots. He looked out the window, where his horse stood. Ruben lifted his tail and let fall a pile of droppings. Then the horse pissed a thick yellow stream into the dirt of the street. A bird twittered outside under the porch eaves.

"Doc, you make sense with what you say. And I do want to remember them as they were in life. And I will. But I want to see what those bastards did to them too. I want to remember every hard blow my father took. The killer must have caught him by surprise and hit him real hard because Pa was a fighter. He would not have let either of those sons of bitches hurt my mother. So I know that much. I know my father was attacked by someone real mean. And for anyone to hit a woman like that, well, that person is not human. He's an animal. I want to see what Wiley and Fritz did to my parents. I want to remember that too."

"Why? Isn't your grief enough, Lew? Aren't your good memories worth more than the pain you'll go through when you see them, see the way they are?"

"No, Doc, it's not enough. I hope the law will take care of those murderers, but I can't count on that. Wiley Pope's father, Virgil, swings a lot of weight in these parts and I think he'll stick up for his boy, maybe send him away. If he does, I may have to hunt him down. If I do, and I catch him, then Wiley will have to answer to the law."

"What law is that, Lew?"

"My law. The law of the gun."

"Lew, you can't take the law into your own hands. You'd be a criminal yourself if you followed your law."

"If the law here hangs those boys, I'll be satisfied, Doc. Otherwise, I'll resort to an older law."

"An older law?"

"He who lives by the sword dies by the sword," Lew said. "Or in this case, he who lives by the gun dies by the gun."

"I've a good mind not to let you go back and see your parents, Lew. That's dangerous talk you're making here."

"You can't stop me, Doc. You got a wagon ready to take them up to the undertaker's in Alpena?"

"It's out back, hitched up. Skip Huckabee is going to drive the team."

"Good. Skip was a good friend to Ma and Pa."

"All right, Lew. Let's go back. Miss Jones did some loving work on your folks. The best she could."

"I'm sure," Lew said, anxious to get it over with, this looking at his dead parents.

Doc led him down the hallway to his office, then back through an examining room, and finally, into another room that was like a closed-in porch and ran the length of the house at the rear. There, on two tables placed end to end, two sheeted figures lay in repose. Seneca turned from the window. There were trees just outside that provided shade in the summertime, but were now gaunt and leafless, lending a starkness to the room that gave Lew the shudders.

Rankins walked over to one of the tables and slid the sheet down to the chest, revealing the face of Lew's father.

"You may not want to see your mother after this," Rankins said.

Lew felt a cold iron ball form in his stomach when he stepped closer and looked down at his father. Yes, Seneca had done a good job. His father smelled of powder and some faint scent of flowers or talcum. But the cuts were there, the bruises. His father's skin had turned dark, a yellowish brown, and he looked waxen. Lew gulped in air and fought down the nausea.

Seneca came up beside Lew and put a hand on his arm.

"Do you want to see your mother, Lew?" Rankins asked.

Lew nodded, struck dumb by death.

Rankins gently removed the sheet from Jenny Zane's face. Lew turned to look at his mother and felt his legs sag at the knees, knees turned to gelatin by the hideous mask that had been his mother's kindly face.

Her visage was one large bruise, and her mouth had been crushed, the lips flattened so that some of her teeth showed. The flesh was taut over her bones and almost translucent. Lew thought he could see her skull beneath it, the beginning of a Halloween grin. It was hard to recognize the corpse as his mother, but he knew it was she. Seneca had put a pretty white dress on her, one with a lace collar, high enough to hide the bruises on her chest and breasts.

But Lew knew how badly his folks had been beaten. Death could not hide the ravages of that murderous attack on their persons. He gulped air to keep himself from swooning, and forced himself to look once again at both his mother's face and his father's.

"You can cover them, Doc," Lew rasped, and turned away.

Seneca squeezed his arm and he looked at her. She was so young, so beautiful, so alive. The contrast was startling, and he had to breathe in more air lest he give way to his wobbly knees and fall into her arms senseless.

"I-I'll get my horse and meet Skip out back," Lew said, and walked from the room, dazed and numb from another attack of overwhelming grief.

Seneca started to go after Lew, but Rankins held her back.

"Let him go, Seneca," he said. "He's got to work this all out in his own way."

Lew heard that and went on through the rooms. He thought he heard Seneca choke back a sob, and that touched him, touched his heart like a healing hand. And maybe, he thought, someone else cared about his folks as much as he did. And maybe there were good people in the world as well as bad.

10

By the time Lew rode around to the back of Dr. Rankins's house, Skip, a large, burly man sporting faded red galluses holding up his gray duck trousers, bracing a checkered woolen shirt, was just finishing up. They had loaded Lew's parents in the bed of the covered buckboard, while Seneca stood by to help. She climbed up in the wagon and made sure the bodies were secure atop the down comforters she had placed inside.

"I'll be right with you, Skip," Lew said. "Got to use the privy before we set out."

Lew dismounted and walked to the small wooden building. Next to it was a crate piled high with dried corncobs, some reddish, some yellowed or brown. He picked up a cob and went inside. Skip held the reins of Lew's horse, and was rubbing the animal's nose when Lew returned from the privy. Seneca and Rankins secured the tailgate on the buckboard. Lew looked inside, saw the bodies resting on two folded-over comforters.

"We didn't have any pine boxes," Rankins said. "But we tried to make the ride as soft as possible."

"That's fine," Lew said.

"Is there anything I can do for you while you're gone, Lew?" Seneca asked.

He took the reins from Skip and walked over to her. Sunlight splashed on her dark hair and her pigtails gleamed with a shining radiance as if they burned with an inner light.

"Do you know Cletus Sisco real well?" he asked.

"I know him. He lives up on Possum Trot near my daddy's farm. He helps with the milking every morning."

"Will you see him later this morning?"

"I might. Cletus and Daddy are making sorghum today. Why?"

It was still cool outside and as the wind freshened, Lew saw that Seneca was beginning to shiver.

"Can Cletus read and write?" Lew asked.

"Yes, I think so. Why?"

"I'd like you to ask him to write out what he saw yesterday at the store. Have him put down the names of the boys. Everything."

"All right. What do you want him to do that for, Lew?"

"If I don't get any satisfaction from the law in Alpena or Berryville, I want to take that paper up to the judge and let him read it."

"Sheriff Swanson rode out early this morning, heading for Berryville, he said. I'm sure the law will act swiftly in this case."

"Well, that's some good news," Lew said.

"But you don't trust Swannie?"

He heard the lilting voices of children floating on the breeze. He looked over and saw boys and girls skipping and hopping on their way to the schoolhouse. Again, he thought, life goes on.

"No, I don't trust any of the lawmen I've met around here. They're a lazy bunch for the most part."

"Lew," Rankins interrupted, "I see you're still packing a pistol. I hope you'll let Sheriff Swanson handle this. Those boys are plumb mean and if you were to go up against them, well . . ."

"I'll give the law all the rope it needs to hang those two killers," Lew said. "But if I run into them first, I don't know what I'd do."

Seneca reared back in shock.

"Lew," she said. "You wouldn't shoot them, would you? Without a trial? In cold blood?"

Lew tied the long reins to the back of the wagon, wrapping them around one of the posts that held the sideboards on and running them through the crack.

"I might," he said.

"Don't you dare," Seneca said quickly, then turned away as color suffused her cheeks. Lew saw that she was biting her lower lip as if to still her tongue.

There was so much Lew wanted to say to Seneca just then. But there were people around and he wanted it to be private. He thought, from the way she acted, that she might have feelings for him, that she wasn't just being neighborly, but might even want him to court her. The way she acted just then . . . It wasn't something he could mull over for a real long time right now, he reasoned. But it was something that he might want to ask her about when they were alone. Whenever that might be.

"All right," he said, acting on a sudden impulse, "I won't do nothing, Seneca. Like you say."

She turned to him and smiled.

Lew felt something melt inside him. It was a feeling that he had never had before. Not with such intensity. He almost felt as if she had reached inside him and was squeezing his heart, caressing it like a woman would do with the petals of a fresh-cut rose when she lifted it up to her nose and closed her eyes to sniff its delicate fragrance. That's what he thought about when she smiled at him. That, and his heart melting from a soft warm touch, or just the sweet breath from her lips.

"I'll do what you ask, Lew. When you come back, I'll

have what Cletus tells me all written out and signed by him."

"Thank you, Seneca." He checked the reins and they were tightly tied. "I guess we better go."

Skip was tamping tobacco into his clay pipe, waiting for Lew.

"Whenever you're right ready, Lew," Skip said. "We got a long ride ahead of us, and best we leave while it's still cool. Might get up to fifty or sixty today."

"Good-bye, Lew," Seneca said. "You take care, you hear?"

"I will. Good-bye, Doc. Thanks. You tell me what I owe you and I'll pay you when I get back."

"We can talk about that later. You just take care of what you have to do with your folks."

Lew started to leave after Skip struck a match and lit his pipe.

"Oh, wait, Lew," Seneca said. "Something I forgot to tell you."

"What's that?"

"Reverend Cobb come by Dr. Rankins's office this morning early and said he wanted to hold services for your folks. With flowers and singing and all."

"When?" Lew asked.

"Whenever you plan to have the funeral in his church. Tomorrow or the next day maybe."

The school bell started ringing. The voices of the children and the laughter began to die away. Like the songs of angels, he thought. Like the lost souls of the damned. The echoes of the pealing bell began to die away too, and he wondered if his folks could hear them, wondered if they could read his thoughts just then. Crazy thoughts at such a time. But their bodies were in the wagon, stiff as dried oak boards left out in the weather.

"I don't hold much with funerals," Lew said.

"Why?"

"I went to some when I was a little kid. My grandpa's.

My grandma's. My aunt Bernice's. My uncle Vestal's. Funerals seem to wring out every last ounce of grief from a person. When Peggy's mother died, you remember her, Peggy was still bawling and hugging her dead mother in the casket, asking her to come back, begging her mother not to leave her. Seeing that just tore out my heart."

"It's a way for loved ones left behind to say good-bye," Seneca said quietly.

"You can say good-bye without no funeral."

"Lew, you're not the only one who'll miss your ma and pa. Other folks knew them, loved them. They'll want to honor them."

"They don't have a right," he said with a stubbornness that surprised even him. He had never expressed his feelings about funerals before with anyone. To him they were a spectacle, a performance by people who tried to outdo each other with wailing and crying and taking on. To Lew, a funeral was a pagan ceremony that neither honored the dead nor comforted the living.

"Yes, they do, Lew. You can't just deny folks a chance to grieve, to hear good words said by a preacher. It just wouldn't be Christian or proper. People might think you were cold and that you didn't care about your folks."

"Let them think what they want."

"Are you dead set against having a funeral for your folks then?"

Lew could smell the smoke from the burning pipe tobacco. He realized that both Skip and Doc Rankins were looking at him, listening to what he had to say. He felt surrounded, trapped. Yet he hated to give in when a principle was at stake. He wondered, though, if he was not just showing his inner bitterness over the death of his parents, being perverse about something so traditional as a funeral because of his anger, his hatred of the two who murdered his folks.

"I reckon I'll talk to Mr. Goodwin up in Alpena about a funeral," Lew said. "Ask him when we could have it. Tomorrow or next day maybe."

Seneca smiled at this small victory.

"You'll feel better about it afterwards, Lew."

"I reckon."

"We better get goin'," Skip said, puffing on his pipe so that his breath fanned the coals in the bowl.

"Well, good-bye, Seneca," Lew said. "Doc."

"When will you be back?" she asked.

"I don't know. Tonight or tomorrow maybe. I hope you get Cletus to write out that paper for me."

"I will."

Lew followed Skip to the front of the wagon. Skip let Lew climb in first, and then he hauled himself up onto the seat.

"Hang on," Skip said as he released the brake and lifted the reins. Two horses were hitched to the wagon, an unmatched pair. To Lew they looked like plow horses, but maybe they'd get them up to Alpena, some thirteen miles from Osage. Skip clucked to the horses and shook the reins so that they rippled over the horses' backs. The horses strained at the harness and the wagon began to move.

When they passed the store where his parents had died, Lew looked at it. Edna would be there in a while to open it, but for now it stood empty. Lew was surprised when Skip halted the wagon right in front of it.

"What are you stopping here for?" Lew asked.

"I'm real sorry about your folks, Lew. I thought you might want a moment to remember 'em."

"No, keep on going. I'm remembering too much as it is."

"Sorry."

That was the thing about death, Lew thought. Nobody knew how to handle it. Skip thought he was doing a good thing, but he was only dredging up terrible memories. He hadn't been there the day before. He hadn't seen what had happened. He hadn't seen the blood, hadn't seen their faces, the horror of it.

"No need to be sorry, Skip," Lew said, his anger cooling.

"I just thought . . ."

"Just forget about it, will you? All I want is to put my folks to rest."

"That all? Don't you want to see those boys that killed them get hanged?"

Lew didn't answer right off. Did he want to see them hanged?

Or did he want to kill them himself?

11

GOODWIN'S UNDERTAKING BUSINESS WAS IN A MODEST CLAP-
board building on one of the back streets of Alpena. It was
just a house, set back off the dirt street, with big oaks and
gum trees surrounding it. But it had a back alley, and Skip
pulled the wagon up there to a makeshift loading platform
that appeared to have been made out of scrap whipsawed
lumber. No two boards were the same width or thickness,
and some of the square nails had started to work out of the
wood over time. There were a number of barrels against
one wall, a storm cellar door on a slant next to the house,
and a pile of tubes and pipes that were turning to rust under
the eaves of the house.

Skip set the brake as a tall, thin, skeletal man emerged
from a back door and stood on the platform.

"What do we have here?" the man said. He wore a vest
over a pale blue shirt and his pinstripe trousers were pressed.
His black shoes were shiny. He wore suspenders, and a pair
of spectacles hung from a lanyard around his neck. His
mouth was small and pinched, as if he had just eaten something sour. The lips looked even smaller under the thin

pencil of moustache under his narrow, aquiline nose.

"We have remains in the wagon," Skip said bluntly.

"Ah, your loved one?"

"Nope. It's his folks." Skip cocked a thumb toward Lew, who sat there sizing up the man on the loading dock.

"You have two corpses in your wagon?"

"They're not corpses," Lew said, rising from his seat and stepping down off the wagon.

"How crude of me. I'm Hal Goodwin. I'm the under-taker here. And you are?"

Lew walked over to the dock.

"Lew Zane. In the wagon are my folks, Delbert and Jen-nifer Zane. They were killed yesterday down in Osage."

"Killed?"

"Murdered," Lew said, a chiseled edge to his voice as he filled the man in on all the details.

"Oh, dear," Goodwin said, and brought a hand up to his mouth like a woman does.

By then, Lew knew he didn't like Mr. Goodwin, and his dislike increased as the morning wore on, with papers to fill out, a promissory note to pay Goodwin for his services, the unloading of the bodies and carting them into a room that smelled of formaldehyde and alcohol.

"Do you know Reverend Cobb at the First Baptist Church of Osage?" Lew asked.

"I do. Nice gentleman."

They were seated in Goodwin's small office near the front of the house. It was as neat as the way Goodwin dressed, with file cabinets, a small cherry-wood desk, a number of chairs with cushions and paintings of serene landscapes, along with a bare cross tacked to the wall be-hind the chair where Goodwin sat. Skip played with his suspenders, pulling them out from his body and then let-ting them go back without snapping against his shirt. That was as annoying to Lew as was listening to Hal Goodwin drone on in his simpering voice about his services, his re-spect for the dead, his experience, and his fee.

Goodwin took Lew and Skip to a small showroom where he had three caskets on display, a simple pine box, one made of teak, and another of mahogany. Lew was already figuring in his head what the burial was going to cost him, and he meant to pay Skip and the doctor, and give the Reverend Cobb some money.

"Now, your loved ones will not last long in the ground if you choose the pine coffin," Goodwin said. "The teak, however, will last for centuries. So too the mahogany."

"The pine box will suit me just fine," Lew said. "Nothing is forever."

Goodwin didn't argue or try to talk Lew into purchasing a more expensive casket. Instead, he wrote down the cost of two pine coffins on a little pad he carried with him.

Back in his office, Goodwin added up the figures and wrote the total out for Lew. He handed the piece of paper across the desk.

"Now, how would you like to handle these expenses, Mr. Zane?"

Lew looked away, stared out the window at the leafless trees on the side of the house. He had a few dollars in a wooden cigar box under his bed at home. His mother always kept some money in a jar on one of the kitchen shelves. He didn't know if his father had put away any money at home. The store money had been cleaned out, and was probably already spent by now.

"I'll try and have your money for you by tomorrow, Mr. Goodwin. Will my folks be ready by then? Reverend Cobb wants to hold services at the church in Osage."

Before Goodwin could answer, they all heard footsteps on the front porch. Then the door opened and someone walked down the hall. A woman appeared in the office doorway. She was all bundled up against the chill, appeared shapeless under all the clothing.

"Good morning, Hal," she said. "Do you have work for me? Oh, good morning, gentlemen. I saw your wagon pull up. I live just across the street."

"Sit down, Sandra," Goodwin said. "This is Mr. Zane, the bereaved, and his friend, Mr. Huckabee. Gentlemen, this is Mrs. Sandra Clarke, who provides cosmetics for the deceased and helps me with reconstruction."

"Reconstruction?" Lew asked, nodding to Mrs. Clarke, who sat down. She had a large carpetbag, which she placed on her lap as if it contained the crown jewels.

"Ah, sometimes the deceased has damage to the facial tissue and bones," said Goodwin. "Mrs. Clarke helps to give the loved ones a more natural look."

There it was again, Lew thought. A mention of someone looking natural after death. Death was ugly. None of the dead people he had seen looked natural in any sense. He wondered if undertakers were taught to lie or if it just came natural. He tried to imagine Mrs. Clarke trying to make his parents' faces look as they had in real life. Could she brush away the scars, cover the bruises, make the skin as smooth as it had been in life? He didn't think so.

"How did your parents expire, Mr. Zane?" Sandra asked.

Goodwin answered before Lew could.

"They were assassinated," Goodwin said. "The Pope boy and young Canby."

"Wiley and Fritz?" Mrs. Clarke said. "I'm not at all surprised it's come to this."

"What do you mean?" Lew asked.

"Those boys," she said. "Always in trouble. Stealing and the like. Why, they're notorious, those two. Wiley especially. Bad seed that one. He beat a boy at school very severely. Nearly killed him. The doctor had to sew several stitches in his head to keep the poor tyke from bleeding to death."

"Tyke?" Lew leaned forward in his chair.

"The boy Wiley beat up was only eight or nine years old. I think Wiley was fifteen or sixteen at the time."

Lew looked at Skip, who shrugged as if he had never heard the story before either.

"What else?" Lew asked.

"Mr. Zane, this is hardly the time. . . ." Goodwin began.

Lew waved a hand at Goodwin. "Please go on, Mrs. Clarke."

She seemed pleased to be the center of attention, much to Goodwin's annoyance.

"Why, those two robbed a grocery over in Green Forest not more than two months ago. They had pistols and scared the poor storekeeper half to death. I think they stole thirty dollars that time."

"That time?" Lew seemed about to leap from his chair.

"Why, Mr. Goodwin, you remember what they did to poor old Mr. Tanner last spring. Wiley shot his dog and when Mr. Tanner ran out to try and save the little critter, Wiley and Fritz beat him with the dead dog. Luke spent near a month in the hospital over in Harrison."

"That's enough, Mrs. Clarke," Goodwin said. "We all know how bad those boys are."

"Were they ever arrested?" Lew asked.

Mrs. Clarke opened her mouth to answer, but Goodwin held up his hand to shush her.

"Wiley's father, Virgil," Goodwin said, "carries a lot of weight hereabouts. He as much as told the sheriff here in town that he'd better not arrest either Wiley or Fritz Canby. I believe, however, that Mr. Pope compensated the victims. Paid them cash not to press any criminal charges."

Lew leaned back in his chair, stunned.

Goodwin cleared his throat.

Skip snapped his suspenders against his shirt and Mrs. Clarke jumped at the sound. Goodwin frowned at Skip.

"There's been some unsolved murders too," Mrs. Clarke said, blurting out the words before Goodwin could stop her. "Mighty peculiar, you ask me."

Lew leaned forward in his chair again.

"Never mind, Sandra," Goodwin said. "You don't want to go making unfounded accusations."

"Let her talk," Lew said. "What unsolved murders, Mrs. Clarke?"

"Well," she said, "there was that Murchee boy down in Carrolton. Somebody shot him dead and then dragged him into the crick. They didn't find him for three days. Everybody thought Wiley done it because they were friends and had a big old argument just before that."

"Nobody accused Wiley of that killing," Goodwin said.

"No. That was the talk, though. And there was another murder, last winter right here in Alpena. Another boy, name of Walton. Went to school with Fritzie and Wiley. Fritz and Jimmy Walton got in a fight and two days after that, somebody shot Jimmy in the face."

"And people think Fritz or Wiley killed him?" Lew asked.

"Wiley was seen going over to the Walton house late that night. Fritz was with him. A neighbor heard Wiley calling Jimmy to come outside, and then she heard loud voices and a shot. They found Jimmy dead right after that."

"Did Virgil Pope pay these people off too?" Lew asked.

"Nothing was ever charged or proved," Goodwin said. "And Sandra, I won't have you spreading rumors to my customers. So you just stop telling tales out of school."

"Yes, sir," Mrs. Clarke said, frowning. She clutched her carpetbag close to her and stared out into nothingness as if thinking over something that was right on the tip of her mind. "But I know what I know and I hear what I hear."

"Enough," Goodwin said. "Mr. Zane, I think our business is concluded here. Your folks will be ready for the funeral tomorrow. I'll come down for it and you can pay me then."

Goodwin walked out from behind the desk and held his hand out to Lew. Lew rose and shook it. Then he turned to Mrs. Clarke.

"Thank you, ma'am. I appreciate your telling me what you did."

"No proof, mind you," Goodwin said.

"I understand," Lew said. "But I'm not the law. Those boys murdered my folks and we've got an eyewitness. They won't get off this time."

Skip rose from his chair and shuffled toward the door.

"You riding back with me?" Skip asked.

"No, I'm going to pay the sheriff a call. You go on, Skip. I'll see you down in Osage later."

"You be careful today, Mr. Zane," Mrs. Clarke said. "Especially when you talk to Billy Jim Colfax."

"Why?" Lew asked.

"Never mind, Mrs. Clarke," Goodwin said, trying to usher Lew toward the door. Mrs. Clarke ignored him.

"Billy Jim might try to fool you, Mr. Zane," she said. "And you surely know what day this is."

"What?" Lew said.

"Why, it's the first day of April, Mr. Zane. April Fool's Day."

She wagged a finger at him and there was a mischievous twinkle in her eye.

"I'll keep that in mind, Mrs. Clarke," Lew said, winking at her.

When he and Skip finally left, Lew felt as if he was carrying a huge weight on his shoulders. And his mind was running like a millrace, the thoughts streaming through it in a silent fury.

12

THE SHERIFF'S OFFICE WAS JUST ACROSS THE ROAD FROM THE Northern Pacific Railway station. Beyond the station and the tracks lay the yards of the Pope Lumber Company. Stacks of lumber rose up like small buildings in a miniature city for as far as the eye could see in both directions. Lew could see men working, driving carts piled high with cut boards, moving in and out of the rows of cured lumber in different grades. Beyond, to the west, actual buildings towered above the lumberyard, and he saw the huge sign emblazoned on one of them: POPE LUMBER COMPANY. On the other side of the yard, he knew, there was a railway siding where cars could come in and load or unload lumber. Up the road, he saw a wagon turning into the company's yard. It was laden with logs for the sawmill, which he could hear humming in a high-pitched whine as logs were stripped of bark on four sides, the sidings sent rolling down a ramp of small wheels and dumped in a pile where workers would remove them and stack them in a separate lot. These slabs were sold to poor homesteaders or farmers who used them for privies, hog pens, and other cheap buildings. He had worked on the green chain, what they called the ramp where the slabs slid down after being sawed off raw timbers, and it was hard work.

Lew reined up in front of the sheriff's office, which was next door to a small café. On the other side of the sheriff's office was the jail and next to it, an attorney's shingle swung in the breeze, and beneath that, another sign that read BAIL BONDS. Neat, handy, Lew thought. Everything you need in one place.

There were benches in front of the courthouse and some of the other establishments. In midblock, a building said COURT on its high face, and at the west end of the block stood the old stage stop, which was now a freight office. Lew saw the name and felt a twinge when he read it: CANBY DRAYAGE. Beneath that he saw the word FREIGHT and beneath that, WE HAUL ANYTHING, ANYWHERE. Seeing the name Canby brought a sharp pang to Lew's innards. Those were probably Canby wagons hauling timber to the Pope Lumber Company.

He tied Ruben to the hitch rail out front and stepped onto the boardwalk that fronted the buildings along the main road. He read the words on the door: SHERIFF OF ALPENA, and underneath: W. J. COLFAX.

A man sat behind a desk, looking out the window at him. His feet were up on the desk and he held a dime novel in his hands. But he was looking straight at Lew, and at his horse. Lew opened the door and walked in, his eyes narrowing to adjust to the dim light. A small fire muttered in the potbellied stove in the far corner. The room was warm, but cooling as the fire died down.

"Sheriff, I'm . . ." Lew started to say.

"I know who you are. Swannie woke me up early this morning and told me you'd probably come by."

"Well, I'm here."

"Set yourself a chair, Zane." Colfax laid the tattered magazine down on his desk, which was cluttered with dodgers and papers. There was a spindle, which held other papers skewered there like dead white leaves. A wooden box with no lid sat on the table and someone had scrawled in black ink the word WARRANTS. The box appeared to be empty.

Lew sat down and looked at Sheriff Billy Jim Colfax, sizing him up by studying his facial expression and his eyes. Eyes that were like chips of obsidian, dark glints sunk back behind high cheekbones like the eyes of a pit viper.

What was it Lew's father had told him? The words streamed through his mind. *You look at a man's eyes, Lew. You can see into his heart, if you look hard enough. You can see into his soul. And his face. It's a mask a man wears, but if you put the eyes and face together, you can read a man like a book. No matter if he smiles and shows white teeth, his eyes and face will give him away if he's not being honest with you or if he has something on his mind other than being friendly.*

Colfax's lips bent in an enigmatic smile. The expression didn't show friendliness or hostility, but was like something pasted on for the moment, something drawn by an actor's pencil across a shapeless mouth. Lew didn't even know if the man had any teeth in his head. The smile was just a meaningless scrawl across the bottom part of his face and didn't even stretch to his sideburns, which were long and curved toward the mouth at the bottom, wider at the bottom than at the top.

"If Sheriff Swanson stopped by, then you know what happened to my folks," Lew said.

Colfax picked up a stub of a pencil and made a bridge between his index fingers. Like a tiny fence rail. He kept the pencil level with Lew's face and looked around one side of it.

"I heard they was beat up some and died."

"They were murdered," Lew said. "Brutally."

"I ain't seen 'em so I can't rightly say."

"What did Swanson tell you this morning?"

"Not much. Just that he was riding to the county seat with his report."

"Look, Sheriff, I didn't come here to beat around the bush all day."

"You look, sonny. I don't need none of your sass and when you talk to me, you keep a civil tongue in your damned head. You hear me, boy?"

"There was an eyewitness who saw the two boys who slaughtered my parents. Slaughtered them like hogs. Swanson say anything about that?"

"He said there was a break-in, maybe, at a little store down in Osage. There may have been a fight. A man and a woman died from injuries. No evidence of what may or may not have been stolen. Nobody knows for sure who broke the latch on the back door. That was about it. He doesn't know who broke in any more than I do, Zane. So my advice to you is to go back home, cool off, and let the law in Berryville take care of this little matter."

"This little matter?" Lew tried to retain his composure. "My folks were murdered, Sheriff. And, as I told you, there is a witness who saw Wiley Pope and Fritz Canby leave the store right afterwards. Those two boys live here in Alpena and you probably know them real well. I hear they've been in trouble before."

"I know those boys. And they were always a little wild. Just boys, though. That's all they are. What do you want me to do? The break-in happened in Osage and you've got a sheriff there, Don Swanson. He's handling the case, if there is a case."

"You could help," Lew said. "You could bring those boys in for questioning, or talk to them about it. It shouldn't be too hard to tell if they're lying if they deny killing my folks."

Colfax swung his feet off the desk and tossed the pencil down. He leaned across the scattered papers and stared straight into Lew's eyes.

"Listen, sonny, you're not the law. You're not an investigator. You weren't there when your folks died. And, for all I know, those boys you mention might just have been passing by, went into the store, saw two dead people, and then took off, scared out of their wits. Swanson said he didn't have any proof that those boys did anything down there. Somebody might have seen 'em, but nobody saw 'em kill anybody."

"That's just shit, Sheriff, and you know it."

"You want some good advice, Zane? Don't try to be a detective. Don't jump to conclusions. Go on back home and let Swannie sort it all out. If the sheriff over in Berryville thinks there's a case, he'll likely investigate real good and maybe he'll arrest somebody. Now, I'm busy and I don't do real good with gossip."

"You know damned well those two boys did what I say they did. They murdered my folks."

"Some more advice for you, Zane. You go messin' around with Wiley Pope and Fritz Canby and you're liable to wind up at the undertaker's yourself."

"Is that a threat?" Lew asked, rising from his chair.

"No threat, sonny boy. Just some good advice. You don't know what you're messin' with here. Those boys come from money and you ain't got a pot to piss in. So get on out of my office or I might have to lock you up for disturbin' the peace."

"What peace?"

"My peace," Colfax said, and his eyes turned to hard agates. The thin scrap of a smile on his face faded like smoke in a high wind.

"I'm leaving," Lew said, "but you haven't seen the last of me. I mean to see that those two boys go in front of a judge and get what's coming to them."

Colfax stood up.

"I see you're packin' a pistol, Zane. I think there might be a town ordinance against carrying a weapon in open

view. You better git while the gittin's good or I will throw
you in jail until you cool down."

Lew knew he couldn't buck Colfax just then. The sheriff was wearing a big Colt Peacemaker and he probably
wouldn't hesitate to use it. There was something menacing
about Colfax, and that badge he wore made him right even
when he was wrong. No, now was not the time to get into a
fracas with Billy Jim Colfax.

Lew slammed the door when he left the sheriff's office.
When he mounted Ruben, he saw that the sheriff had his
feet back up on the desk and was holding the dime novel in
front of his face. But he was looking out the window to
make sure Lew was leaving.

"Bastard," Lew muttered under his breath, and swung
Ruben around, started him up the street. "Busy my ass."

He rode up the street, feeling like an outcast, a pariah.
He certainly could not expect any justice in Alpena, maybe
not even in Berryville or Osage. The weight of it all was
beginning to crush him, and yet he knew he must not give
up hope that Wiley and Fritz would face a court of law and
be punished for the crime of murder. But just then, everything seemed hopeless and he was far from home.

He passed Cushenberry's Hardware Store and the
Alpena Mercantile. People were on the boardwalk, peering
in windows, carrying goods they had already purchased. At
the end of the block, he slowed as he came upon the building that housed Canby Drayage. A woman was outside,
sweeping off the steps and boardwalk. She looked up at
him, a curious look in her eye. Lew recognized her. He had
seen her at school with her son, Fritz, when both Lew and
Fritz were small. He reined up in front of her.

Sarah Canby looked up at Lew, paused in her sweeping.

"Mrs. Canby," Lew said, touching the brim of his hat.

A look of puzzlement flickered on her face like a vagrant shadow.

"Are you one of the new wagoneers?" she asked. She was
dressed well, and warmly, with a shawl over the shoulders of

her long woolen dress. He could see her heavy stockings just below the hem and above the tops of her lace-up boots that seemed made of fine leather.

"No'm. I'm Lew Zane. I went to school with Fritz."

"Oh, my, you've grown," she said. "Yes, I remember you now. You're Jenny's boy."

"Yes'm. Is Fritz around?"

Another look came onto Sarah Canby's face. Her eyes narrowed to a suspicious squint.

"Fritz? Why do you ask?" Her tone had changed from friendly to curt.

"I was going to talk to him about something."

"About what?" She had turned belligerent.

"I was going to ask him why he murdered my ma and pa yesterday morning, ma'am."

"Get out of here," she snapped. "Get out of here or I'll have my husband give you a sound drubbing. You'll not make false accusations to me, young man. Now get."

Lew touched two fingers to his hat in a polite farewell.

"I'll catch up with Fritzie later," he said, his tone light-hearted. "You tell him that, Mrs. Canby."

She took the broom and raised it over her head as if to strike at something. Her glare was hotter than the sun that beamed down and struck Lew's face as he rode away, keeping sight of her out of the corner of his eye. As he headed for the road south to Osage, he saw her turn and dash inside the building, slamming the door behind her.

By nightfall, he figured, it would be all over town that Lew Zane was a troublemaker.

Well, maybe he was.

Or soon would be.

13

WILEY STIRRED THE COALS WITH A STICK, MOVING THEM around the shallow fire pit so that they changed colors. He knocked ashes from one and revealed a portion of its glowing eye. It looked like an eye to him, a blood-filled eye energized by an inner fire. The coals hypnotized him as they always did. They brought a sense of peace and tranquility to him. They always did when he poked at them or blew breath upon them so that they pulsed and flared like angry eyeballs. He liked the way they gave off heat whenever he disturbed them with his blowing breath. As if they were alive.

Next to him, on the floor of the cave, his pistol lay on a soft cloth, reeking of gun oil, the blood scoured away, the bluing on the barrel once again shiny and clean. He liked to look at the pistol, a Colt, with its smooth rosewood grip, its barrel so pure and straight, the cylinder snug and filled with cartridges, a heavy solid thing, with the power to kill. He didn't put it back in its holster because he wanted to be able to look at it and to grab it up if the need arose. He loved the smell of the oil too, the way it mingled with the smoke from the coals, taking away the dank aroma of the cave.

He heard the horse picking its way up to the creek, and he dropped the stick onto the coals and crawled to the entrance. The stick moved slightly as the hot coals began to dry it out. Wiley thought that it looked alive, that it looked like prey for the coals. Soon, they would eat the stick alive, make it burst into flame, and all the coals would flex and pulse with renewed energy.

Wiley peered from the cave, keeping low. He heard the horse's hooves slosh into the creek. The iron shoes scraped over stones and made a small clattering sound like a jawbreaker rolling over his lower teeth.

As Wiley watched, Fritz clapped both heels into his horse's flanks. The horse bounded from the creek in a single jump, splashing water on the bank. The hooves rang on stones and sparks flew like tiny winking fireflies as iron scraped against flint and rock. Wiley frowned as the horse climbed the bank, sending a small avalanche of dirt and pebbles back into the stream. These vanished with a gurgle that sounded like someone swallowing a bucket of water in one gulp. The murky track disappeared as the dirt broke up and washed downstream, reduced to silt.

"Fritz, you make enough noise to wake the dead," Wiley said.

"Whooeee, have I got some news for you, Wiley."

"Well, put that damned horse up with mine and get back down here."

"That's why I'm a-hurryin'," Fritz said, a gap-toothed grin giving him the look of an imbecile.

Wiley turned back to the cave in disgust, crawling to his former spot, where he found comfort in picking up his Colt and holding it in his lap. The weight of it on his leg gave him reassurance that the news Fritz was bringing, along with some eats, would be good, not bad.

The cave was on property owned by Wiley's father, Virgil. It had always been a favorite place for Wiley, and this is where he and Fritz had come after leaving Osage. It was inside a small bluff above a stream Wiley had named after himself, calling it Wiley's Creek. Behind a knoll above the limestone outcropping, his father had built a small corral and a lean-to. This was where Wiley and Fritz kept their horses. It had originally been used to house the mules that plowed the field beyond where Virgil had grown hay when he was a young man. The family no longer grew hay on the one hundred acres and the field had gone fallow and weedy, was full of snakes and field mice and quail. Wiley thought it was a good hideout because it lay above Alpena but was behind a long high hill, unnoticed and forgotten by most of the townspeople.

Wiley heard Fritz clamber back down the slope on foot. A moment later Fritz entered the cave, lugging a flour sack full of groceries. They could stand up in the cave, but had to hunch over a little, so they seldom stood. Fritz dropped to his knees and crabbed the few feet to where Wiley sat. He glanced at the pistol in his friend's lap.

"You going to shoot somebody, Wiley?"

"Don't be a smart-mouth, Fritz."

"Well, you got your gun out and all."

"I cleaned it."

"Again?"

"What'd you bring us?"

Fritz grabbed the sack at the bottom and pulled it up, spilling its contents onto one of the blankets they kept in the cave.

"A whole bunch of stuff."

Wiley snorted as he picked through the crackers, dried beef, a wedge of cheese, some airtights with peaches and pears, some hard candies, two more candles, wooden matches, sardines, and four licorice sticks.

"You done good, Fritz."

"Wait'll you hear, Wiley."

Fritz scooted into a sitting position on another blanket and put his hands over the coals as if to warm them. All of the snow had melted that day, but it was still chilly, and getting chillier as the afternoon waned.

"I'm waiting," Wiley said, a sarcastic whine to his voice.

"That Zane boy was in town today. Ma saw him come to the drayage. She talked to him."

"She talked to Lew Zane?"

"Yep." Fritz grinned. "He asked where I was and Ma told him to git." He chuckled. "Run him off."

"Lew came lookin' for you?"

"Sure did, and Ma said he went to see Billy Jim too. He's a-lookin' for both of us."

"Your ma told you this?"

"Sure did."

"You didn't run off at the mouth, did you? You didn't tell no one?"

"Hell, no, Wiley. You know me better'n that. I didn't tell a damned soul 'bout what we done."

"Are you sure your ma talked to Lew Zane? I mean, she still thinks 'maters are poison."

"She does not."

"Does too."

Wiley picked up another dry stick from the pile of wood stacked against the cave wall and stirred the coals, then dropped the small branch into the pit. He watched the coals pulsate and waited for the stick to catch fire.

"So, what did Zane tell Billy Jim? Did your ma tell you that, Fritz?" Wiley's tone thickened with sarcasm.

"That Zane said they was an eyewitness what saw us murder them old people."

"Who?"

"Somebody named Sisco, Ma said."

"Clete Sisco? That bastard don't have all his marbles."

"That's what Ma said. Sisco seen us. Zane didn't tell Billy Jim the name, but he got it from Swanson."

"How much of that twenty did you spend on these foodstuffs, Fritz?"

"Nary a Indian-head penny. I got all this from home."

"So, nobody knows you got money in your pocket."

"Nope. I done what you told me, Wiley. I didn't say nothing to nobody. And I don't remember seein' that Sisco feller anywheres around that store."

Wiley put some wood on the fire. It was getting chilly inside the cave as the sun fell toward the western horizon. There was a hole in the top of the cavern, so the smoke rose toward it. Both boys had explored the cave, some of it. It went back into the limestone for quite a distance and then branched into several passageways. They had always been afraid to go beyond that point, but Wiley had always wondered if one of the passages might come out somewhere else, and he was constantly riding his horse to other places looking for a similar cave. He had never found a different exit to the cave, but he kept hoping that he would.

"We were in such a hurry to get the hell out of Osage, no tellin' who all saw us down there."

"One thing, I reckon," Fritz said. "Billy Jim ain't hot on our trail."

"Did you work today?" Wiley asked.

"Nope. Pa said he didn't need me. You?"

"Naw. My daddy told me to sober up and help my ma." Wiley started giggling. So did Fritz. They rolled around on the blankets, their eyes streaming tears from the laughter.

"Any of that whiskey left?" Fritz asked, wiping his eyes.

"Yeah, two full bottles. But you ain't drinkin' none of it."

"How come?"

"We got to think about that witness."

"Huh?" Fritz blinked away the last of the tears.

"We don't need no witness to what we done," Wiley said.

"No, I reckon not. What you wanta do, Wiley?"

"Let me think. You bring the makings?"

Fritz fished in his pocket, pulled out a sack of tobacco and some papers. He tossed them to Wiley, who slid a thin paper out of the folder and creased it with his finger. He worried the pouch open with his little finger and poured tobacco out into the paper trough. He pulled the string on the pouch with his teeth, closing it, then folded the paper over into a roll, licked the edge to seal it, and stuck the cigarette in his mouth. He picked up a box of matches and struck one. He puffed on the cigarette, then tossed pouch and papers back to Fritz.

Fritz put the makings back in his pocket and pulled out a cheroot and lit it.

"Why didn't you tell me you had seegars?" Wiley said.

"I forgot."

Wiley slapped Fritz on the side of the head. Fritz recoiled and snatched the box of matches from Wiley's hand. He lit his cheroot and the two boys smoked and built up the fire. Wiley put his pistol back in its holster, patted the butt. They crawled outside the cave to look at the sunset.

The western sky streamed with salmon banners of clouds hovering above the horizon. The creek burbled with a soothing sound.

"You feed the horses, Fritz?"

"I put grain in the bins for both of 'em."

"I wonder where this Sisco lives down there in Osage."

"Dunno. Why?"

"We can't just let him walk around blabbing about us."

Fritz shook his head. "No, we can't. Pa would likely give me a stropping if he knew about what we done down there."

"You're dumb as a lop-eared mule, Fritz, you know that?"

"What do you mean, Wiley?"

"You got a lot more to worry about than a licking from your old man."

"My ma?"

Wiley snorted in derision. He looked at Fritz as if his friend had lost his mind entirely. He shook his head.

"You like that neck of yours, Fritzie?"

"Huh?"

Wiley brought a hand up to his own neck and squeezed it with his fingers.

"What you and me got to worry about is getting a rope around our necks."

"Huh? From who?"

"From the law, you dumb mule. Haven't you never heard of hangin'?"

"I heard of it."

"Well, if anybody believes that Sisco sonofabitch, they might hang us."

"Who?"

"The law, that's who. Fritz, sometimes I wonder if you've even got a brain. If you do, it sure as hell don't work well."

"Oh, I ain't worried none about the law," Fritz said.

"No? You ain't worried at all, are you?"

"Oh, yeah, I'm worried, Wiley."

"About what?"

Fritz drew on the cheroot and blew a plume of smoke into the air. "That kid Zane. He's lookin' for us, and Ma said he was wearing a pistol. A big old Colt like your'n."

Wiley froze as if he had been struck with a lightning bolt.

"You know, Fritz, maybe you ain't as dumb as you look. Yeah, we sure got to worry about that Zane boy. I remember Lew from school. He was a quiet one. Them are the ones you got to worry about. The quiet ones."

And they sat silent as the sun set, both of them thinking about Lew Zane, trying to remember what he was like when last they saw him, and thinking about what they would do when they saw him again.

14

BY THE TIME SENECA ARRIVED BACK HOME THAT MORNING, the cane that had been stored all winter in their silo, having been cut and trimmed, was stacked in wagons lined up near the mill. It seemed to her that most of the people who lived up on Possum Trot were there in the yard, eager to help her father in the making of sweet sorghum.

Seneca put her horse up in the stables and joined her father, who was just closing up the silo. Ed Jones was a short, sturdy man in his forties with gray streaks in his dark brown hair, gnarled hands that showed the effects of hard work and sun, fingernails constantly black from years of digging in dirt and working on machinery. His blue eyes were framed by deep wrinkles that gave him a kindly look, despite his wooden, austere countenance.

"You're just in time to stoke up the cook fires, Seneca," Ed Jones said as he dropped the wooden bar into its cradle.

"Weren't waiting for me, were you, Pa?" she said.

"I had Clara," he said with a laconic smile. "She can burn syrup good as you."

"That's not fair, Daddy. I only burned one small batch last year."

"The sweetest batch of all," he teased.

She took his arm and shook it as they walked toward the mill. The mule was in harness to the pole, standing there, head lowered, one hind leg cocked hipshot, its tail switching like a metronome.

The sun had not been risen long and it was still cool up on the ridge top. Seneca greeted the women and the men as she and her father walked toward the wagons. She smiled warmly at their friends and they smiled back. The women clucked to one another about their sewing and quilting and churning, while the men swapped winter stories of ice and snow and hunting, as folks will do who have not seen one another for a long while. There was the heady tang of spring in the air and everyone seemed to have the fever, long before anyone had spotted the first robin.

"Where's Cletus, Pa?" Seneca asked as she loosed her grip on her father's arm and drifted toward the cook pots.

"Yonder." Ed pointed to the woodshed. Cletus was bent over picking up logs and sliding them onto a stack in his cradling arms.

"I'll start the fires pretty soon," she said. "I want to talk to Clete first."

"We'll get started pretty quick too. Still waiting for a couple of people to come down out of the hills yet."

Seneca looked around at the milling crowd, peering at them more closely to see who they were. Before, they had been a sea of faces, a flock of coats and hats and leggings, bonnets and fur pieces, so familiar, in a sense, that she felt no need to identify each individual, but now she was curious about who was there and who was still missing from the throng.

There were the Millers and the Smiths, the Gleasons and the Davises. She saw Tommy Burrell, her old boyfriend, and he seemed almost a stranger to her now, with the pants he had outgrown showing the whites of his ankles, the brown coat seemingly shrunk to a smaller size on his gangly frame, the woolen cap like the top of an acorn, with its moth holes and dangling strands of dark thread. He smiled and waved at her, and she smiled back, but it was like looking at an old tintype that had faded with time, faded and blurred so that she just barely recognized him as a one-time acquaintance.

And then she realized that she had been looking for Jenny and Del Zane and their handsome son, Lew. Not consciously, of course, but longingly, and from an old habit she scarcely recalled she had, of always looking for them at sweet sorghum-making time, early in the spring of every year. It seemed now that she saw their ghosts among the crowd, shadows of them alongside familiar faces, their backs to her so that she could not see their eyes and noses and mouths. Her heart tugged with an unseen pang as if a delicate hand had squeezed it just for a second, and she turned away quickly to deny sight of the phantoms, to quell the memories that swelled up in her mind and threatened to make her weep from a sudden, inexplicable, and profound loneliness. Of course, Lew Zane was not there, and she shouldn't have expected him to be, but neither were his dead folks, and she had known they would not be there. It was only a trick of the light and a quirk of memory that made her look for them, and see them, or their shadow selves, amidst the crowd of neighbors who seemed unaware that good folks were missing from their gathering and would never be seen again.

Her mind snapped back into the present as she forced herself to walk toward Cletus Sisco, who was piling the wood he had gathered up next to the cook pots, and there was Clara Neely standing there, a muffler wrapped around her neck like one of the burlap sacks used to filter the syrup, her cheeks stung to a pale rose by the cold so that she looked like a caricature of a puppet in a Punch and Judy show.

"Clara," Seneca said cheerfully when she approached

the woman, "would you so mind starting the fires and tending them for a while? I need to talk to Cletus."

Clara brightened like the golden petals of a sunflower when Seneca asked her to do something she already dearly wanted to do, and she smiled with a seldom-seen radiance as if Seneca had bestowed upon her, a mere charwoman, the mantle of a princess, or a queen.

"Why, Seneca, my dear, you know I will," Clara chirped with her birdlike voice. "Just you go about your business with Cletus and leave the chore to me. Oh, I can't wait to smell the sugar from the cane on such a bright spring day. Now don't you worry none; I won't burn a speck of sorghum syrup. I know just what to do."

"I'm sure you do, Clara, and thanks so much," Seneca said, wondering how she could politely escape Clara's outstretched arms that wished to clasp her in an embrace. At the last moment, she realized there was no escape and she endured the quick hug, the cloying smell of powder on Clara's body seeping through her clothes like fine dust blown from a bellows.

Seneca reeled backward from Clara, forcing a smile.

"You just run along now, dearie," Clara said with a patronizing air. "Just leave everything to your aunt Clara."

Clara was not her auntie, but a lot of the folks who lived on Possum Trot referred to her in that manner, including Seneca herself.

"Cletus, can you come up to the house with me?" Seneca said, tugging at Sisco's elbow.

"What for?" he asked.

"I'll tell you when we get there."

Cletus beamed at this attention, and he followed Seneca up to the house at the top of the sloping yard.

"You just wait out here on the porch steps, Cletus, and I'll be right back."

"Yes'm, Miss Seneca. I'll set right here." He sat down as Seneca bounded up the steps and into the house. She returned a few moments later with some blank papers, a breadboard, and a sharpened pencil. She sat down beside Cletus, leveled the breadboard on her lap, and set the papers down, tapping them into a neat pile with her hands.

"What you got there?" Cletus asked.

"Can you read and write, Cletus?"

"Some. I ain't none too good with ciphering, but I can write some and I been taught to read. I don't cotton to big words, though."

"Can you sign your name?"

"Why, sure, Miss Seneca. I learnt that in fourth grade. Or was it fifth?"

She smiled. "That's all right. I want you to talk to me about what you saw at Del and Jenny's store. I'm going to write it all down and then you're going to sign it for me. Would that be all right?"

"I don't know. I reckon. Long as it's you doin' the writin'."

She poised the tip of the pencil over a sheet of blank paper. "Just tell me what you saw that morning, Clete."

"I seen two horses tied up down to the crick," he said. "I was checkin' my muskrat traps early and was comin' back home, two rats in a sack. Then I seen the horse and buggy what belonged to Jenny and Del up by the smokehouse. I walked up yonder, curiouslike, and heard an awful racket when I passed by the back of the store."

Seneca was writing furiously, but Cletus was talking slowly, so she had no difficult writing down what he was saying.

"Go on," she said.

"I started to go in the back door, when I seen the latch was broke. So I went over and hid ahind the smokehouse. Right after that, I heard some noise and peeked over at the back door and seen these two boys come running out. They was stuffin' paper money in their pockets and one of 'em, Wiley Pope, had blood all over his hands and clothes. They run up the crick and got on them horses and lit out for Carrolton lickety-split like they was on fire. That's all I seen until I went inside the store. The back door was left open. Then I seen poor Del and Jenny lyin' there dead and all bloody. I run and got the sheriff. Swannie and me come back to the store and he liked to puke when he saw Jenny and Del."

"What were the noises you heard, Clete?"

"Godawful noises. Smackin' sounds and moanin' and such. I was plumb shakin' in my boots."

"Do you know who the boys were?" she asked. "The ones coming from the store?"

"Yes, I recognized them," he said. "It was Wiley Pope, Virgil's boy, and Fritz Canby. I have seen them at the Blue Hole and they used to steal from my muskrat traps when they were small. Those are bad boys."

"But you didn't actually see them hurt Jenny and Del?"

"Naw, I didn't. But I heard those noises and there was nobody else in the store. It was them all right."

"That's good, Clete. Is that what you told Sheriff Swanson?"

"Yeah, I told him who I seen."

Seneca looked down and saw that the mill was loaded with cane and the mule was walking its circular path. The mill turned and the juices were squeezed from the cane. The fires were going under the sorghum pans, and Clara poured the juice into one of them as it poured from the mill.

"Just sign here, Clete," Seneca said, moving the paper around to face him. She handed him the pencil. Clete signed his name, Cletus A. Sisco.

"The A is for Albert," he said.

"That's fine, Clete," she said. "You can go on back down now and help Daddy."

"Yes'm. I done told all this to Sheriff Swanson and he wrote it down too."

"Did you sign what he wrote down?"

"No'm, he didn't ask me to."

As Cletus walked back down the slope, Seneca took the papers back inside the house. She could smell the syrup cooking when she came back out. She joined Clara and stirred the syrup in one of the pans. Her father came over, took the wooden ladle from her, and dipped it into the syrup.

"When the sugar's high enough," he said, "you take it off the fire, hon."

"How can you tell when it's ready, Pa?" she asked.

He smiled. "I got a sweet tooth. Your ma had a better one."

A shadow of sadness clouded his eyes when he said that. He turned away and walked over to another pan.

The whole process, she knew, would take two hours or better, and they would all pour sorghum molasses into clay jugs, cork them, and her father would give each of the helpers a jar of the thick molasses to take home with them. There would still be plenty left over for Seneca and her father and to sell for the Zanes' store. When she thought about them, she felt her throat constrict. Tears welled up in her eyes and she took deep breaths to keep from crying out loud in front of everybody.

The syrup was thickening and the smell of it was overpowering. She looked around at all the people, laughing and talking, teasing her father, and she thought about the Zanes, Del and Jenny. They were not there that day, but she saw them anyway, felt their presence, and shivered from a sudden chill. Her blue eyes glittered in the sunlight as fresh tears flooded her eyes. She bowed her head so that Clara would not notice. But she caught her father's eye. He was looking at her and he was nodding.

She knew he understood.

15

THERE WASN'T MUCH TO CARROLTON. IT WASN'T EVEN A TOWN really. There was a house by the side of the road, dusty from the passing wagons and horses, a few farmers beyond the creek and the trees, hidden from view. Yet there was always a lingering sadness about the place that Lew felt every time he passed by and remembered the Fancher family and the other families who had encamped there before leaving for California.

He rode to the creek to let Ruben drink and thought of those hundred and twenty-odd people from Carroll and Marion counties stopping there at that very same spot before heading for Utah and their deaths. It was early in September in 1857 when they departed from Carrolton. They never reached California and by the following year, they were all dead, massacred at Mountain Meadows by Mormons. The shock of that massacre still lingered as well, for several children were also killed.

Ruben slurped water through rubbery lips and the bit clacked against the horse's teeth. Lew sat there, looking down at the creek that was running fleet from the melted snow, its waters dappled by sunlight, its banks still wet, the mud spongy. Ruben's front hooves sank in the loamy soil and his tracks filled with murky water.

Lew heard the sound of hoofbeats and turned in the saddle. He knew who the rider was even while he was a small silhouette coming down the road, his horse at a trot, the natural gait for that breed of Missouri horse. Don Swanson's trotter was a fine animal, sixteen hands high, black, with three white stockings and a small star blaze on its forehead. Sunlight glinted off the badge on Swanson's vest, shooting beams of light in all directions.

Good timing, Lew thought, and watched as Swanson left the road and headed down into the meadow toward the creek. He looked weary as he rode up and his horse, Nox, slowed, whickered at the sight of Ruben, or perhaps at seeing the creek and smelling water.

"Don," Lew said.

"Afternoon, Lew." Swanson gave Nox his head and the horse stretched its neck and nibbled at the stream, snorted, then moved closer to slake its thirst more easily.

"You been to Berryville," Lew said.

"Yep. You take your folks up to Alpena?"

"Me and Skip hauled them up to Goodwin's."

"I'm right sorry still, Lew. I mean it."

"I know you do, Swannie. You see the sheriff over yonder?"

Swanson nodded.

"And? Is he going to arrest those boys?"

Swanson's horse finished drinking and Swanson reined him back away from the bank. Lew turned his horse so that the two men faced each other on horseback. Ruben pawed the ground with his left forehoof. Lew patted the horse on the neck. A bobwhite quail toodled in the thicket beyond the creek, its plaintive call slicing through the silence.

"I saw Rudy Cooper. And I talked to Judge Wyman."

"What did Rudy say?"

"He was half-drunk," Swanson said. "Old Rudy gets started early with John Barleycorn."

"He ought to arrest himself."

"I bought him some coffee and we talked for a spell."

"Damn, Swannie, getting information out of you is like getting seed ticks off a Persian cat."

Swanson reached into a shirt pocket and took out a plug of Day's Work. He worried a Barlow pocketknife out of his pants pocket, opened it, and cut off a chunk of tobacco, stuck it in his mouth. He tongued it to one side of his jaw and began chewing on it.

"Rudy listened fine until I told him Sisco seen young Wiley Pope and Fritz Canby come out of the store afterwards, stuffing paper money in their pockets."

"Then what?"

Swanson shrugged. "Then he said 'thouten Sisco actually seein' the killin's, he didn't think I had enough evidence to arrest those two boys."

"Bullshit, Swannie."

"He said I could talk to the judge, but he wasn't going out of his way to rile Virgil Pope and Luke Canby."

"He's afraid of them?" Lew asked.

"Ah, well, I don't know about being afraid. Virgil's married to Rudy's sister."

"I didn't know that. But being kin shouldn't make any difference. My folks were murdered by those two boys and they ought to be in jail right now."

"Lew, you headed back to Osage?"

"Yeah."

"We can talk on the way. I've got to get back. Been gone most of the day."

They rode across the meadow toward a connecting road, not talking. Lew had a sick feeling in his gut. He dreaded hearing what Judge Ringgold Thaddeus Wyman had said when Swanson talked to him. From the way he was acting,

Lew figured Swanson had gone to the well and found it dry as a year-old gourd.

They passed a marker that someone had put up, honoring the memory of those pioneers who had journeyed from this place to their death in Utah. Swanson and Zane both glanced down at it.

"Gives you a spooky feelin', don't it?" Swanson said.

"Yes," Lew said. "All those people. Women and children. Did you know any of them?"

"My folks knew some, the Dunlaps and the Fanchers. They still talk about it as they get up in years."

"There are so many stories about it. Some say the Mormons thought the people who set out from here had killed some of them."

"Wasn't true. Paiutes attacked the Mormons when they were heading out for Utah. Warn't any of Fancher's party. They were all peaceable people."

"They were all wealthy too," Lew said. "That's what I heard."

"My daddy said they had money. Alexander Fancher, they called him Piney Alex, had been to California two times before and when he left Carrolton, he had his own family with him. They had forty wagons, something like seven hundred head of cattle, and amongst them about seventy thousand dollars in gold."

Lew whistled at the large numbers as they rode past the marker.

"Didn't Alex Fancher have an expensive horse too?"

"Yeah, a stallion worth two thousand dollars. You know, they even had a doctor with them. Some of the women were widowed and they had their families with them. I think about forty families in all."

"So senseless, murdering all those people," Lew said.

"Fancher never saw it coming. He always resupplied from the Mormons whenever he went that way, but that time, Brigham Young refused to sell them any goods. My daddy said there was an argument broke out and Brigham set out to do them all in. Him and the other Mormons made up stories about the wagon train, saying they poisoned one of their cows and some Injuns ate the meat and died. They also said Fancher's people were poisoning the springs as they passed through. Warn't none of it true."

"Fancher got to Mountain Meadows after he left Salt Lake City and that's where everyone died. Was killed."

"Yeah, good grass there. But they camped some distance from water, I heard, and Injuns attacked them and kept them away from the water. Then some white men came up under a flag of truce and said they'd help them."

"But they didn't," Lew said.

"Tricked them, was what they did. Anyway, all of those who went with Piney Alex died, got killed, and the Mormons done it."

"Senseless," Lew said again. "So damned senseless."

"Like what happened to your folks, Lew."

"I was thinking that."

"It don't do no good, though."

"Don, you were going to tell me what the judge said when you told him about my folks."

"Yeah, well, I met with Wyman and laid it all out for him. I even told him what Rudy Cooper said. I said I wanted to arrest Pope and Canby and bring them into his court for trial."

"What did Judge Wyman say?"

"I don't know if I should tell you all this, Lew. It sure ain't going to help none."

"I want to know what I'm facing, Don."

Swanson spat a stream of tobacco juice out of the side of his mouth. It splattered into the mud of the road. They reached the main road to Osage and headed south on it. The road was wet with snowmelt for as far as they could see. Ahead, the hills rose up like islands, the bare trees among the green looking skeletal, as if they were ancient ruins, signs of devastation and death.

"Judge said I could arrest those boys and he'd try them. But he said they'd surely get off."

"Get off? Why?"

Swanson sighed as if he were dealing with a child's inane questions.

"Money, Lew. Wyman said it greased the axles of the government's wheels."

"Money?"

"Virgil Pope and Luke Canby would hire a high-dollar defense lawyer for their boys."

"So? The county's got a competent prosecutor, doesn't it?"

"A feller name of Mike Farris prosecutes for Carroll County. He's good enough, all right. Maybe better'n most. He's young and smart and got him a law degree from Columbia, up in Missouri. He wins cases for the county, Wyman says."

"But Wyman doesn't think he'll win against a high-dollar defense attorney," Lew said.

"It ain't only that," Swanson said, and Lew could tell he was keeping something back, reluctant to tell him the whole story. "There's other things, ah, considerations, I reckon."

"What other considerations?"

"Likely, Wyman says, Pope will start showing money, handing out greenbacks to him and Farris and anybody else connected to the trial."

"You mean Wyman would take a bribe?"

"He don't call it that. Way he puts it, the government runs on money. Judge don't get no big salary. Neither does the prosecuting attorney. So, when money comes in to them, they look at it like an extra salary and they look the other way, so to speak."

"They look the other way?"

"The boys get off, or get light sentences. Slaps on the wrist."

"That's just shit," Lew said. "That's just not fair. What about justice?"

"I asked Wyman about that."

"I can't imagine what he said about that."

"Let me see if I can get it right. Wyman said that justice was an abstract concept that had no meaning in the everyday world. He said it was an ideal and that each person had his own idea about what justice was. The court can be satisfied with a resolution to a case and call it justice, no matter what. Those on the other end might call it an injustice. Wyman said it was all in the way you mix it."

"The way you mix it?"

"He said that sometimes the greater good must prevail. He told me that to keep peace and harmony in the county and not upset any apple carts, he might have to let Pope and Canby prevail. That's the way he put it. He said that both men, and he was talking about the daddies of those two boys, contributed to the greater good of the county. That's what he said."

"Those boys are murderers and my folks weren't the first of their victims."

Swanson snorted. "You know that?"

"That's what I hear."

"Judge said the same thing. He said in every barrel there's bad apples. And we just have to live with the spoilage, hope that justice will find another way to work."

"What did he mean by that?" Lew asked.

"He didn't say. But I thought that he meant either that the boys would grow up and stop being criminals, or move away to another county and become somebody else's problem, or . . ."

"Or what?"

"Or maybe," Swanson said, "somebody would kill them."

"Who?"

Swanson shrugged. "Not me."

"And if I killed them?"

"You'd hang for sure, Lew. Less'n you got more money in your pocket than Virgil Pope or Luke Canby."

"So, there is no justice."

"Not in this world. Fact is, Judge Wyman said that very thing. He said it was an old expression among lawyers."

Lew's eyes narrowed to slits as the anger inside him began to swell and build and rise up in him like some gathering force that had no name. There had to be a way, he thought, to bring Wiley and Fritz to trial and see that justice, true justice, was served.

The problem was, he did not yet know how to go about accomplishing that. And he did not want to wind up being branded as a killer, or dangling from the end of a hangman's rope.

16

SHERIFF SWANSON LIVED BELOW THE HIGH BLUFFS ON THE other side of the Zane property, closer to Alpena. He and his family had a large apple orchard there, sold cider and apples at a roadside stand, but also shipped their product to other parts of the country. In fact, Canby Drayage hauled apples for the Swansons to Fayetteville, Rogers, Little Rock, and other places in Arkansas, as well as to Springfield, Kansas City, Joplin, and Jefferson City in Missouri.

That was where Swanson and Lew parted company that dark day of sunshine and thaw and bad news. Swanson left Lew with a last piece of free advice, and it added weight to the burden Lew already carried on his shoulders since leaving Alpena.

"You don't want to mess in something you can't handle, Lew. Virgil Pope is a powerful man, and some say he's a mean man. No wonder he sired such a bad one as his son, Wiley. But you can't beat men like Virgil. He owns Alpena and he owns Osage. And, some say, he owns even the souls of people who work for him and live with him. Just go on and live your life and let God take care of Wiley and Fritz. They won't be goin' to heaven and you can take satisfaction that they'll burn in hell for what they done to your folks."

"Thank you, Don. I know you mean well and I'll consider what you say. But I have different ideas about heaven and hell from what the preachers preach."

"Vengeance is mine, sayeth the Lord."

More preaching, Lew thought. But he didn't tell Swanson what was on his mind as he waved good-bye to the well-meaning sheriff. He watched Swanson ride up the lane past apple orchards on both sides, bare-limbed trees stark against the brooding bluff beyond and the green hills folding in on the back side of his farm, their slopes bulging with fragrant cedar trees that stayed verdant the year round and grew to sizes that made for good furniture at the hands of a finished carpenter, chests and wardrobes and jewelry boxes that sold for high dollar in the big cities.

Lew struggled to piece together all of the information Sheriff Swanson had given him. He could expect no help from the county sheriff or the county judge. They would either do nothing about the murders of his folks, or they would be bought off by Pope and Canby. It was all very discouraging. His only hope was that Seneca had gotten a signed document from Cletus Sisco that would prove who killed his folks and force the judge and prosecutor to try and convict Wiley and Fritz, send them to prison or to the gallows. One thing Lew was sure of. He would not give up, despite the obstacles in his path.

He dreaded going by the store his parents had owned, but there was no way to avoid seeing it again. Edna Butterfield might still be there, and that might help, to see someone alive working at the store, someone friendly at least. He had to face up to that, the same as he had faced going home to an empty house last night. There were two vacant places in the universe where his parents had been, but their ghosts still lingered, like wisps of spiderwebs clinging to an old abandoned barn, or forgotten lyrics to some barely remembered song he used to sing as a child.

As Lew rounded the ridge that led up to the high bluffs, he saw the store, expecting it to be dark and lonesome in the fading sunlight, like that place in his heart where he kept his memories of Del and Jenny like musty letters in an attic trunk. The road lay in shadow, for the sun had fallen behind the high hills to the west, and there was a chill on the road that the sun had abandoned, a chill that stole through his clothes and clawed at his bones with icy fingers.

He saw something fluttering on the porch, something bright and out of place, as if it had blown there and become attached to one of the pillars holding up the roof. As he drew closer, he saw more of them, flapping from both pillars, some looking like dark scarves, others bright red or orange, and one green, another a saucy yellow like some shred of sunlight left dangling in the wind that blew at his back and past him down the deserted and darkening road.

Small figures darted across the porch, banged in and out of the front door. Raced around the store, shrieking and laughing. Children. Some came up to the porch carrying streamers in their hands and Lew saw them wrestle with the ribbons, then tie them to the posts before dashing away again, their laughter trailing after them like echoes in a sleeper's dreamscape.

As he drew closer to the store, Lew heard the streamers rustling in the wind, crackling like bacon sizzling in a pan or making a flapping sound like small whips, and he saw that the streamers were made of crepe paper, the kind the schoolkids used to decorate their dances and their fairs.

Curious, Lew rode up to the hitch rail out front and dismounted. He wrapped the reins around the pole and stepped onto the porch. When the children who were there saw him, they shrieked in mock terror and scrambled away, around the side of the building, disappearing like elfish creatures vanishing into a Celtic wood.

Lew grabbed one tyke by the arm before he could escape and whirled him around. He pointed to the crepe streamers.

"What is all this, son?"

"Mister, I didn't tie none of them," the boy said. He must have been eight or nine. "Let me go."

"What's your name, sonny?"

"I ain't done nothing," the boy said.

"I didn't say you did. I just want to know what all this means. If you know, you'll tell me, won't you?"

"I don't know. It's for the licorice at two-for-a-penny, I guess."

The boy pulled loose from Lew's grip and clambered across the porch to the end, jumped down, and flew around the corner and out of sight.

Lew looked down and saw flowers in pots arranged along the baseboard of the front wall, and notes with flowery scrawls and drawings stuck into the spaces between boards, and a wreath made of grapevines leaning against the wall, wrapped with white ribbons as if for some festive occasion.

Puzzled, Lew opened the door and walked inside. The bell tinkled overhead, but nobody paid him any mind. The store was full of people, all chatting and talking at once, it seemed, and Edna standing behind the counter, her hair askew, uncoiled ringlets dangling over her ruddy cheeks. She was making change for two ladies with children tugging at their dresses and babbling for some treat that Lew could not decipher.

He stood there, dumbfounded, having never seen that many people in his folks' store before. And they all seemed to be buying something, a small trinket, candy, a can of baking powder, a skillet, a book, cookies from a jar, and he smelled sorghum when he looked at a row of earthen jugs atop one counter, all appearing to have been freshly corked.

And then Lew saw Seneca at the back counter, reaching up to a shelf while a clutch of women looked on, as if eagerly awaiting what she would bring down for them. And women stood in line with spools of thread and packets of sewing and darning needles, and some of them looked at him askance as if he had intruded upon some private ceremony in which they were the only participants.

Edna looked up, saw Lew, and smiled wanly. He nodded to her and made his way through the throng to the back counter, where Seneca had finished her retrieval of a set of canisters and was taking paper money that was shoved at her by one of the women.

Lew waited until Seneca was finished with her transactions, then moved to the counter, edging away other women looking at the goods in the display cases. Seneca smiled when he appeared before her, her blue eyes sparkling with a radiance that told him she was glad to see him. He smiled, glad to see her too.

"It's been like this all afternoon," she said. "Folks coming from all over to pay their respects. The kids. Did you see what the kids did?"

"I saw," he said.

"I've never seen anything like it. It's as if folks wanted to pay their respects to your ma and pa in the only way they knew how. Poor Edna's been working herself to the bone."

Lew glanced over at Edna, who seemed to be holding her own. Now, many of the women, and there were men there too, were giving him shy, sidelong glances, and a lot of the talk lowered into whispers.

"I'm bowled over," Lew said. "I didn't expect anything like this. I thought people would stay away in droves because of what happened here."

"Even the doctor came in, and the foreman at the plant. I've seen people here today that I haven't seen since the Fourth of July."

She spoke with a breathless passion, her eyes shining

with wonder as she looked at all the people buying goods.

"I don't recognize half of them," Lew said.

"How did your ride to Alpena go, Lew? Did you see Mr. Goodwin?"

"Yes. The funeral will be tomorrow, I reckon."

"Do you want me to tell Reverend Cobb?"

"Would you, please?"

"Tomorrow afternoon all right? Say around two o'clock? That should give most of the folks time to plan and get here for the services. A bunch of people asked me about it today, wanting to know when the funeral will be. Folks want to pay their respects. Your folks were very much admired."

"I knew they were liked some," he said.

"The kids adored them. I don't know if you know this, but many times your ma would sell them candies and such even if they didn't have any money. I think they gave credit to an awful lot of people too."

"Why do you think that?"

"Just asked Mrs. Butterfield. Edna said a lot of people came in saying they owed money and wanted to pay off their debts."

"Maybe they feel guilty they didn't pay my folks when they were alive."

"That's not very charitable, Lew. I don't think that at all. They could have just kept quiet about the money they owed and nobody would know the difference. I mean, now that your folks are no longer here."

"I guess I'm not in a very charitable mood right now," he said.

She put a hand over the counter and touched his arm.

"Did you see the sheriff in Alpena?"

"Billy Jim won't do anything. I saw Swannie too, after he went to Berryville. Seems I'm bucking Pope and Canby and nobody wants to get into the matter of justice."

"Oh, that can't be," she said. "I'm sure something will be done to punish Wiley and Fritz."

"Did you talk to Cletus?" he asked.

"Oh, yes, I almost forgot. He gave me his eyewitness account and I had him sign the document. I can bring it to the funeral tomorrow, if you like. I left it at home."

Lew thought about it.

"Is it pretty clear that he saw those two right after they killed my folks? I mean did he see anything that proves their guilt?"

"I don't know, Lew. Honestly. I think you'll have to show it to a judge or a prosecutor."

"That's just what I aim to do. I'm going to show it to a couple of sheriffs too."

"You look worried," she said. "Is there something else you're not telling me?"

She was very perceptive. He didn't know just then how much he wanted to tell her, or even how much he should tell her. He decided it was best not to worry her. Besides, he hadn't yet talked to Virgil Pope or Luke Canby. He wanted to find out for himself if they would protect their sons at all costs. Perhaps these murders would make the old men realize that their sons were bad and needed to be taught a lesson. Maybe not hanged, but put in prison for a long time.

"No, Seneca," he said. "There's nothing else right now. I've still got a lot to do. If I don't come by your place tonight, would you bring that paper Clete signed to the funeral tomorrow?"

"I will," she said. She paused and looked into his eyes. "I hope you will stop by tonight, though. I'd love to just sit on the front porch and talk to you."

"I'll see. There are things I have to do at home. I can't promise."

She squeezed his arm, then withdrew her hand.

"I'll wait up for you just the same," she said, and there was promise in her words, something that told him she wasn't just being kind or neighborly. The way she said it tugged at his heart, and was the first good feeling he'd had all day. If there hadn't been a flock of people in the store right then, he thought he might just walk around the counter, take her in his arms, and squeeze her tight. He might even try and kiss her.

The promise was there.

He could feel it.

17

The sunset forged flaming clouds in the west, burnished them to a high crimson sheen, gilded them with
gold, then turned them all to ashes against a salmon sky
that lingered into a winter twilight with its soft gray dusk
and whippoorwills calling lonesome into the night.

"Life ain't about money," Edna said as she laid out the
day's receipts on Lew's kitchen table, "but we took in a
heap of it today. All because of the love your neighbors had
for your folks."

"I never seen so much money before," Twyman said.
"Lord, Del and Jenny would have loved to see such grati-
tude and generosity."

"I expect they know," Lew said, his voice husky with
emotion.

Edna looked at Lew in startled amazement.

"Why, Lew, I didn't know you harbored such thoughts.
About an afterlife, I mean."

"Because I don't go to church."

"Well," she said.

"I think life goes on in some form or another," Lew said. "My pa didn't, but Ma sure did."

"Your pa didn't believe in life after death?" Twyman said.

"Nope," Lew said. "Dead is dead was what he believed. But I think he was wrong."

"Hmmmph," Edna snorted. "Well, he's sure found out different, ain't he?"

They all laughed.

"Take your pay, Edna, out of that money, and Twyman's."

"Now, don't you worry none about that, Lew Zane," Edna said. "We'll settle up at the end of the week, like always. I just didn't want to leave this money at the store, seein' as what happened and all. Me'n Twy will do just fine. Now, I can make you a nice supper before we go on home. Lord knows there's plenty here to eat."

"No, Edna, please. I'm not that hungry and I don't want anything fancy. I just don't have the heart to eat tonight."

"No, I speck you don't," she said. "But don't you go wastin' away on me." She smiled a motherly smile.

"I won't. I'm going to go through some of my folks' things and go to bed early."

"Oh?" Edna said with a sly smile on her face. "I thought you'd be ridin' up to Possum Trot tonight, a box of candies in your saddlebags, Lew."

Lew blushed and shook his head.

"Now, why would I ride all the way up there in the dark and all?" he said.

"I saw the way Miss Seneca Jones was lookin' at you today. And you, Master Lew, oh, you were like a big ol' bass a-dancin' on the end of a line."

"I . . ."

"Edna," Twyman said, "you oughten to be teasin' young Lew about sparkin' the gals at such a time."

"Well, I s'pose not," she said. "But Seneca stopped by to talk with me before she left the store this evenin', and she said she so hoped you would drop by her daddy's tonight."

"She said that?" Lew asked.

"Now, would I make up such a story? I swan, Lew. Don't you trust nobody?"

"I did say I might ride on up there tonight, but I don't know. It's an awful long way and I been on horseback most the day. I'm kind of tired."

"You suit yourself, Lew, but that gal's got her heart set on you."

Lew blushed again.

"Funeral's tomorrow afternoon," he said, looking down at the coins and paper money stacked on the table. "At least now I can pay the undertaker and the doctor."

"You keep that money in a safe place now," Twyman said. "You just never know."

"I will," Lew said with a wry smile. "You two go on home. Twy, I hope you can stop by tomorrow, and Edna, don't open the store until after the funeral. If you want to. Otherwise, you can open it the day after if you still want to mind it."

"I do. I don't expect it will be as lively as it was today, but I surely loved being a storekeeper." She looked at Twyman with a knowing twinkle in her eye. "Maybe that's my calling," she said.

They all laughed and Lew said good night to them, watched them walk out the back door into the lingering twilight with the nightjars singing them on their way as if they were sojourners from another country. And then there was a silence in the house, except for the ticking of the wood as it cooled.

He left the money on the table and walked into the front room. He knelt in front of the fireplace and started crumpling up old newspapers, twisting them into tight spirals. He added kindling atop them, laying the sticks across each other and building a small pyramid-shaped stack. He struck a taper and lit the flared ends of the twisted newspapers and fire flared up, licking at the dry kindling wood. As the pyramid flamed, he began to stack logs on the grate behind, and placed a small log atop the fire just in front of the grate. When the fire was burning well, he stepped back from the heat and adjusted the flue as smoke rose up the brick chimney.

He lit a lamp and walked into his parents' room, where he set it on a table next to the bed. It was the first time he had been there since they had died. He felt a rush of emotions as he gazed at the bed so neatly made by his mother on the last day of her life. There was not a wrinkle in the comforter and the pillows were freshly laundered, scented with a faint fragrance that might have been roses.

He could not bear to look at the bed for more than a moment and turned away, his gaze roving the floor. There, beneath his feet, was the woven rug that lay on the hardwood, its colors faded, but it too was clean. He pulled it aside and saw the trapdoor his father had built there. It fit flush against the flooring and had showed no trace of its presence when the rug had lain flat upon it. The handle was a countersunk brass ring that he lifted as he knelt down. The door came open and he felt around the box underneath until he found a metal cash box he knew they kept there. He lifted it out and held it toward the lamp on the bedside stand as he opened it. There was money in it, but he did not count it. He went back to the kitchen and placed the money Edna had brought in the cash box, placing the paper slip with the amount written on it atop the stack of bills.

He put the cash box back in the hidden compartment. He stood up, picked up the lamp next to their bed, adjusting the wick for maximum light. He went to the small rolltop desk his mother kept in one corner, took the key from the nearby shelf, and opened the desk. He rolled the top back and looked in all the cubbyholes, found a key in one of them, hidden from view inside a jewelry box full of meaningless trinkets. He took the key and opened one of the drawers, the one where he knew his mother kept all the important papers.

His mother had told him where to look if she should
die. She had told him a long time ago, but had constantly
reminded him of the drawer containing important family
papers. She had never given him a hint of what those papers were, but had told him that he should find them and
read them. Apparently, even his father hadn't known about
the locked drawer. Or, if he had, he'd never mentioned it.

There was a thick envelope, which he picked up. He
tipped it toward the light and read what his mother had
written on it.

"To be opened after my death," it read.

With trembling fingers, Lew opened the envelope, breaking the wax seal and prying the flap away. Folded inside
were several different kinds of papers, the top one a printed
document with a cover that read: "Excelsior Surety Company, Harrison, Arkansas." He lifted the cover and saw the
names of his parents, the insured, Delbert George Zane
and Jennifer Floy Zane (née Reynolds).

Lew let out a sob when he saw that each of his parents
were covered by a surety bond in the case of their deaths of
$25,000 each. His eyes blurred with tears and he could not
read the rest of it, but only glanced at the scrawl of signatures on the very last page, theirs, and some others, including a notary public as witness to the signing.

He set the insurance policy aside and saw a letter from
his mother. It was addressed to him in her neat, patient
handwriting, the script entirely legible, with each letter
carefully drawn, the words flowing across each line with
symmetrical precision.

He wiped the tears from his eyes and read the letter.

Dear Lew:
If you're reading this, I know that I have left this world.
I've always wanted to tell you how your daddy and I came
to name you, but I did not want to go against your father's
wishes. It was he who named you and, after he told me the
story, I agreed that it was a good name, part of your family's

history, scandalous though it may have been at the time. I do not know all of the story and I don't think Delbert does either, but this is what I've managed to piece together from what your father told me that beautiful day when you were born.

As Delbert tells me, the Zanes came to Ohio during pioneer days. The place was a wilderness when they came there, inhabited by savage Indians, and there was always trouble with the French and the English. One member of the family was Betty Zane, and she had a friend who was a notorious backwoodsman. This man watched over her and the Zane family. He often provided them with food by leaving a freshly killed deer on her doorstep, or bringing them partridges and turkeys he had shot. He protected them from Indians too. Your daddy said his name was Lewis Wetzel and so we named you that, Lewis Wetzel Zane. But Delbert said that was not his true name, but one the family used to disguise his real identity, for he was a famous man among the settlers and the Indians. The French called him *"Le vent de la mort,"* which means "Death Wind" in their language. It was said that whenever he was about to attack renegades or Indians, that a wind always came up and folks didn't know if he made the sound of the wind himself or if it was really wind that blew through the trees. Lew Wetzel was quite a legend, according to your father.

It was rumored that Betty Zane fell in love with Lew Wetzel but that they never married. It was also rumored that she had a child, and your father believes that he is descended from that offspring.

From all accounts your father and I were able to gather, a girl was born to Lew Wetzel and Betty Zane. That child, whose name is unknown to us, later married one of the Zanes. There was no official record of this child's birth in Zanesville. Your father and I checked. But one of your ancestors married a woman identified only as Charity, with no last name listed in any of the official records. We believe that Charity was the offspring of Betty Zane and Lou Wetzel. The family never spoke openly about it, but that is what your father believes. He thinks that Betty's child married a Zane, which would have been incestuous, of course, and that your father is descended from that union. So, you are a true Zane, but you also may be a descendant of Lew Wetzel. You may carry the blood of this famous, and from all accounts kindhearted, man. Your father is proud of his heritage and so am I. And I hope you will be as well.

So, I tell you all this now, so that you will know a little something of your heritage and bloodlines. I know you will carry yourself well throughout life because of the way your father and I raised you.

I love you now, Lew, and I will love you always. You are part of me and you will always be in my heart.

The letter was signed, "Your loving mother."

Tears flooded Lew's eyes as he laid the letter down and leaned back in the chair. The room swam and quavered as he turned to look at the bed once again, as if expecting to see his mother rise from it, walk over to him, and put her hands on his shoulder.

The legend did not mean much to him now, but that one part about Lew Wetzel kept rising above all of the other items he had read about Betty Zane and Lew Wetzel.

That was the part about the wind, the wind the French called "The Death Wind."

He felt the chilblains crawl up his arms, and there was a tingling in his spine just then.

He was sure that he had heard that wind, felt it against his face. It seemed to spring up every time he hunted, just before he killed the game in his sights.

It was curious. It was eerie.

And Lew could not explain it, any more than his mother could.

18

LEW SAW TWYMAN EMERGE FROM THE MISTY WOODS, SILENT as a wraith in his faded gray overalls, a rifle resting on his shoulder. Lew was shaving outside at the well, shivering in his long underwear and regretting he had not filled a bowl and taken his beard off inside the house. But this ritual was a habit he had learned from his father, and Lew's father was very much on his mind.

"Never miss a sunrise, son," his father had told him. "And never miss a sunset. Those are the glories of each livelong day."

Since then, Lew had followed his father's advice and never regretted it. "It gives you a whole new way of looking at the day," Lew always said, "and a nice way to start off an evening."

"Morning, Lew," Twyman said as he walked up.

Lew finished scraping his face with the straight razor, rinsed off the blade, and set it down. He dowsed himself with water from his bowl and dried his face with a towel, picking up shreds of lather on his neck and behind and in his ears.

"You're over early," he said.

"I know you got a lot to do, so I thought I'd help you with the chores. Me and Edny want to spruce up for the funeral this afternoon. I was wondering if I could borry your buggy and mule."

"You can, Twy, and you can hitch up Red Fox if you want. That mule might be too slow for you."

"I'd be much obliged. I got a wheel loose on my buggy and these cold mornings keep my old mule stove up. Rheumatiz, I reckon."

"Let me get some clothes on and we'll feed the stock and then you can hook up the buggy and Red Fox."

"I can tend to the stock, Lew. You got a lot to do in town, I speck."

"Well, thanks. It does look like a long day for all of us."

Lew dressed, got money out of the cash box, and by the time he was ready to ride into town, Twyman had finished the chores and was hooking up Red Fox to the buggy. It felt odd to see the buggy again, but Lew drew in a breath and got over it.

"I see you brought your rifle, Twy. See any squirrels or rabbits on the way over?"

"Nary. A mite early. When the red buds pop and the dogwoods bloom, the squirrels will be down out of their dens, I reckon."

"You get that deer meat?"

"I sure did, Lew. Me and the missus thank you kindly."

"I'll see you in church, Twy."

As Twyman drove off down the lane, Lew threw the blanket on Ruben and saddled him. By then, the stock had stopped blowing steam and the sun was warming the land.

"So pretty on such a sad day," Lew said to Ruben, just to be conversing with something alive and saying what was in his thoughts. He did not relish going to the funeral because he knew everyone would be looking at him, and at each other. People enjoyed public displays of grief, just as they enjoyed public hangings.

He wore his best suit, black as coal, and a black hat with a cardinal feather, in the band. He had polished his good pair of boots and wore a blue shirt and string tie, also black. He took his pistol along, but put it in his saddlebag, out of sight in its holster, the gun belt wrapped around it like a coiled snake.

The town was quiet except for the stave factory with its rumbling of machinery, of belts and pulleys making its wooden walls shake. Wagon loads of lumber waited in the yard, and those wagons that were empty stood outside waiting for drivers to take them back up to Pope Lumber in Alpena. Lew headed for Dr. Rankins's home and office, Ruben shying at the noise from the factory until Lew settled him down with a few words and pats on the neck. He tied up outside and walked through the front door.

"Come on in, Lew," he heard Rankins say. "I saw you ride up."

Lew walked back to the office. Dr. Rankins was sitting there, going over patients' charts, making notations on sheets of paper, then sliding them into folders that were stacked in front of him.

"Sit down," he said. "I've been catching up on my work on this quiet sad day. You're in early."

"I wanted to pay you what I owe, Doc, and see Reverend Cobb."

"Skip Huckabee left a while ago to go with the wagon to bring your folks down. I guess Mr. Goodwin told him to come back this morning."

"Yes, I think so."

Lew felt awkward, out of place. The doctor's office didn't give him the same feeling he'd had at Goodwin's, but he could not scrape death out of his mind. Even though his parents hadn't died in the doctor's office, they had been there and he thought of them now, lying in the back room on tables, almost unrecognizable because of their brutal wounds.

"You don't owe me anything, Lew. I just performed what might be called a humanitarian service."

"You did more than that, Doc."

"Please, let's just forget about it. How are you holding up?"

"I'm fine. I miss them."

"Of course."

"I'm still looking for justice."

"You mean those boys who murdered your folks. Any luck there? I haven't talked to Swannie since he came back from Berryville."

"It seems nobody wants to arrest or prosecute Wiley or Fritz. Scared of their fathers, I reckon."

"Virgil Pope is a hard man to buck," Rankins said.

"I keep hearing that. He should have no say-so in this. His boy is a murderer, old enough to pay for his crime. Same with Luke Canby."

"So, what do you plan to do?" Rankins asked.

Lew let out a long breath and looked out the window, his mind racing over unplowed fields of thought. As always, when faced with a hard decision, he thought back to his father and some of the things his old man had taught him, or said to him. He usually found the answers to his questions in those memories.

"My pa said something to me once, Doc. He was talking about it a long time ago, but it stuck with me."

"What was that?" Rankins asked.

"He said that back when the frontier was raw and folks were just settling and making up their communities, there was no law. And even after some settlements were thriving, there was very little law. He said that when there is no law, or when the law is not working for the people, then someone has to step up and become the law."

"You mean taking the law into your own hands."

"Yeah, Doc. He said that too."

Rankins leaned back in his chair and formed a roof with his hands. He looked at Lew and smacked his lips. He canted his head and squinted one eye as if he was aiming down the barrel of a rifle.

"Do you know what a vigilante is, Lew?" he asked.

"No. From my Latin, it's probably someone who watches. Like a lookout, or something."

Rankins chuckled. "That's probably the original meaning. I studied Latin too. But there's another meaning for a vigilante and it's like what your father told you. It's someone who takes the law into his own hands."

"It's probably not legal," Lew said.

"Well, I don't know about that. But I come from Texas and a few years ago we had us some vigilantes down there. They caused quite a few heads to wag and stirred up a lot of talk."

"So, there was a bunch of them," Lew said.

"The ones I heard about, before the war, were composed of regular citizens. Texas is a big state and there were not a lot of jails nor a lot of lawmen. So, in some places the citizens formed what they called 'vigilance committees.' They became the only law. Sometimes it was for the good of the community, but sometimes these vigilantes used their organization for revenge or for political power."

"What about those that did good?"

"The first I heard of happened back in 1857. Some vigilantes hanged seven horse thieves at different places along the San Antonio River. The vigilantes put the thieves' guns and clothes at the bottom of the trees where they hanged them in their underwear."

"Justice," Lew said.

"Maybe. But in another case, this was in '69, down in Richmond, vigilantes broke into the jail and hanged a horse thief being held there. They took him to a bridge on the Brazos and hanged him from one of the spans. I guess those boys couldn't wait for regular justice."

"Justice moved too slow for them maybe," Lew said.

"Most of the time, the vigilantes would warn the evildoers to get out of town and move on. And if the culprit didn't follow that advice, the vigilantes went after them and served up justice at the end of a rope."

"Well, I don't plan to do anything like that with Wiley and Fritz," Lew said.

"Maybe not. And it's certain that nobody around here is going to buck the law."

"Why not?"

"It's a different time. There is law here in these Ozarks hills. Maybe not the best law, but law-abiding citizens rely on the sheriffs and the courts."

"What if the sheriffs and courts don't do their jobs?" Lew asked.

Rankins collapsed the steeple he had made with his hands and rocked forward in his chair.

"Then some people get away with murder, Lew."

There was a silence in the room. Lew could hear the ticking of the Waterbury clock on the doctor's wall. Rankins sighed as if he had made his point and would not offer any advice. Lew was glad of that. He had a lot to think about, most certainly. Rankins could not solve Lew's problems. Maybe *he* couldn't solve them either.

"What about justice, Doc?" Lew asked after a time. "Don't the people care about justice? Hang the law. Justice is what the law is for, right?"

"On paper, yes. But justice is an ideal. It's not concrete. It's not anything you can take out of a drawer and hand someone. You know the statue of justice?"

Lew shook his head.

"It's a bronze statue of a lady holding a sword in her right hand. In her left hand, she holds up a set of scales," the doctor said. "Justice is supposed to balance those scales. Weighing the crime against the punishment, weighing the deed against the offender."

"That sounds about right," Lew said.

"Does it? I left out one part about that statue, Lew."

"What's that?"

"The Lady Justice is wearing a blindfold."

"I don't understand. Why? Why put a blindfold on justice?"

"Because the law is supposed to be impartial. Because justice is supposed to be blind. And it most often is, of course."

"So Lady Justice is blind," Lew said. "But that doesn't mean the law has to be blind too."

Rankins chuckled. "You've got a head on your shoulders, Lew. And a good mind in that head. No, the law is supposed to have both eyes wide open. Only justice is blind. Blind, but fair."

Lew sighed. "Where is this statue of Lady Justice?" he asked.

"I don't know where the original is," Rankins replied. "Probably in France or England. But there are replicas in nearly every courtroom in America."

"I guess I've never seen this statue or heard of it," Lew said as he rose from his chair. "Well, you've given me a lot to think about, Doc. I still wish you'd let me pay you for taking care of my folks."

"Never mind that," Rankins said. "I know you have a lot to think about. I just hope you make the right decisions as you pursue justice for the murders of your folks."

"I hope I do too," Lew said, and walked out of the office.

There was that weight on his shoulders again. He hadn't given up. He would take that statement Seneca had gotten from Sisco and show that to the law, the judge in Berryville even, and maybe that would turn the tide and bring justice to Wiley and Fritz. No, he had not given up yet, but he wished Osage had a vigilance committee.

He was getting mighty impatient.

19

AS LEW LEFT THE DOCTOR'S HOUSE, HE HEARD THE HIGH-
pitched whine of saws coming from the factory. The sound
rose above the clank and clatter of machinery, the whipping ripple of belts and pulleys. He wondered how people
could work in such a din, and realized he had never thought
much about the making of barrel staves before. Now, of
course, he knew that those noises were making money for
Virgil Pope, and he felt an anger building in him again.
People he knew were working for Pope, and his son was a
murdering coward, still running free while Lew's own parents were about to be put in the cold ground.

He shook off those thoughts, knowing they would do
him no good on such a day. He rode toward the church, at
the far end of town and above the open meadow. He
glanced at the store his parents had built, knowing it was
empty. He wondered how long it could last without his
folks tending to it. Edna could not hope to continue working there. He'd either have to close it or find someone else
to mind it. Someone he could trust.

Percy Cobb was outside the church, sweeping the steps with a straw broom. He looked up when Lew approached, grinned that idiotic grin of his, and waved one hand, then quickly brought it back down to the broom handle. Somehow, he managed not to miss a stroke and the dust flew in two directions.

"Howdy, Lew," Percy said. "Pa's inside, getting things ready. He's just about to rehearse the choir."

"I won't be but a minute, Percy. I'll tie up out back and go in the back door."

"That'll be just fine. Be a heap of folks here this afternoon. For your folks and all."

Lew nodded and rode around to the back of the little church. He glanced at the cemetery on the other side. His folks would not be buried there, but he needed to find out something from the Reverend Cobb.

He tied Ruben to a hitching post the church provided for its congregation and climbed the steps, opened the back door. He heard voices from inside the church, walked past the office and vestibule and onto the small stage. There were a half-dozen women and two or three men standing on one side atop a raised dais, looking at Cobb. They were all holding hymnals in their hands.

Cobb turned around when he heard Lew approach.

"Ah, Lew, come to hear the choir practice?" he said.

"No, Harlan. I wanted to ask you a question, if you don't mind."

"Why, of course, young man. Herb, you all hum the opening to number 192. I won't be a minute. Gladys, don't play the organ just yet."

Lew saw the woman seated in a dark corner behind the choir. Gladys Kunkel, a longtime friend of his mother. She nodded to him and smiled. He nodded back and smiled. Cobb took him by the arm and they walked back to the vestibule, a small room with an open, doorless wardrobe, with smocks and robes on hangers, a small altar on a table with a large Bible atop it, various trays and bottles of grape juice, boxes of soda crackers, idols and crosses on shelves that lined one wall.

"I sent Skip up to Alpena before dawn. Your folks should be here before noon. I'll have everything in readiness by then, Lew. Ah, the caskets will be closed, due to the, ah, the condition . . ."

"That's fine, Harlan. I'm sure you'll do everything right. I need two men to go out to the York cemetery and dig the graves and I need to talk to someone about markers."

"I wish you'd reconsider and have your folks buried in our cemetery," Cobb said. "It's so much more convenient and better tended."

"No, they wanted to be buried there, next to their home."

"I see. Fine then. I have two men coming over who said they would dig the graves for you. They should be here at any minute. They're good men. You know them, I think."

"Who?" Lew asked.

"Bobby Gleason and Kevin Smith. They more or less volunteered. But they're experienced. They've dug graves before."

"I know. They dug my brother's grave."

"Why, yes, little Davey's grave. I remember. So tragic to die so young."

"What about someone to engrave some stones or markers for their graves."

"Oh, dear. You'll probably have to go to Alpena or Green Forest to find someone. There is someone up there in Alpena. I can't recall his name at the moment. The stonemason in Green Forest is very good, though. His name is Wilbur Jennings, I believe."

"All right. I'll be going up that way tomorrow or next day. Thanks, Harlan. I guess that's it. I want to pay you for conducting the service, though. Can you tell me how much it is?"

Cobb cleared his throat. "Ten dollars. We'll pass a collection plate, of course."

Lew reached into his pocket, pulled out a ten-dollar bill. He gave it to Cobb.

"Thank you, my son."

"I'll wait outside for Kevin and Bobby."

"Will you take them to the York cemetery?"

"Yes. I want to show them the plots my folks picked out."

"Lew . . ." Cobb reached out and put a hand on Lew's shoulder. He assumed an air of confidentiality. "I know this is a difficult time for you. And I've been praying for you."

"Thank you, Harlan. Much obliged."

"You're not religious, are you?"

"No, I reckon not." Lew felt his insides squirm at the question. But he met Cobb's gaze and did not feel any shame at his answer.

"May I ask why? Your folks came to my church."

"I have a church I go to, Harlan. It suits me."

"Oh, may I ask where?"

"The woods. That's where I feel at home with the Creator. I listened to a lot of preaching when I was growing up and I just couldn't swallow all that fire and brimstone. When I'm in the woods, when I look at nature, I see how perfect everything is and I can't see a vengeful God, nor even an angry one."

"Still, there is only one God, Lew. And I take my sermons from the Bible."

"They had an arbor church here before you came and built this church, Harlan. Everybody sat outside under the trees and you could hear the birds singing and the wind blowing and it was better than a choir."

"The church has often worked under primitive conditions."

"I read history books too, in school and at home, and it seemed to me that all the wars and troubles were caused by religious folk. The Crusades, the Inquisition, even the Civil War here."

"The Civil War was caused by slavery, Lew."

"Not to hear the preachers, it wasn't. They come through here, so my folks told me, preaching one way or another, for and against slavery, and my pa couldn't make no sense of it. Neighbor against neighbor. Missouri was Union and Arkansas was Confederate. He said he saw more bad things in that war than he ever wanted to see, and all the time people were praying to God and asking Him to slay the enemy."

"People have opinions. They often differ on such matters, Lew."

"I noticed that. Seems to me that a man can go off by himself and sit under a tree in the woods and form his own opinion of things. My pa saw the sense in that too, and he quit going to church."

"So I noticed."

"Well, I don't want to get into an argument with you, Harlan. You preachers are always talking about the people in the congregation as being your sheep. Well, I ain't no sheep and I don't follow real well. So, I go my own way."

"Going your own way can lead to big trouble down the road. Men need guidance. Faith. Men need to follow God's law."

"Seems to me that men make the laws and they don't always uphold those laws."

"God's law prevails over man's."

"So you say. I haven't seen any proof of that."

Cobb shook his head as if he was listening to a recalcitrant child, to a sinner who had gone astray.

Lew held up his hand so that Harlan would not offer more argument.

"Your choir is waiting, Harlan. I'll see you at the service."

"Why, if you don't believe in my church, are you holding the funeral here?" Cobb asked.

"I don't really know," Lew said. "I believe in prayer. I pray. In my own way. My folks are dead. I think maybe other folks want to say good-bye to them in this church. I'll say good-bye to them in mine, when I'm alone, out in the woods, under God's sky."

Harlan opened his mouth to say something, but Lew turned and walked away. He went out the back door and into the sunlight. He had been suffocating inside the vestibule. He was suffocating inside his Sunday-go-to-meeting clothes too. He wished the funeral was over and he could be at the grave of his parents, by himself, to honor them, to bid them farewell, to pray for their souls in his own way.

Harlan Cobb meant well, and Lew thought that he was probably a good man with good intentions. But, as Lew had told him, he was no sheep and he was not a good follower. Whether he was right or wrong, he didn't know. But he believed that man was born with free will and he needed to know how to rely on himself, not on some preacher who shouted and raved about sin and salvation to a bunch of people sinning every day but Sunday and then hoping, in church, that God would save them from hell.

Percy walked around the corner of the church, carrying the broom.

Lew walked over to the hitch rail and leaned against it.

"You waiting for someone, Lew?"

"Yeah. For Bobby and Kevin."

"Oh, the gravediggers, I reckon. You want some help?"

"Nope."

"Pa won't let me dig no graves."

"Oh, why not?"

"He says I'm the son of a preacher and it wouldn't be dignified for me to be diggin' graves."

"Dignified for you or for him?"

"I guess I don't rightly know. I guess for him. He has his reputation to uphold."

"Yeah. Mustn't get dirt on his hands, right?"

"What are you drivin' at, Lew?"

"Nothing. I guess I'm just in a bad mood this morning."

"Well, don't you be sayin' nothing bad about my pa."

"I wouldn't think of it," Lew said, trying not to be sarcastic.

They heard the organ playing the introduction to a hymn, and then the choir began to sing "Shall We Gather at the River."

"Well, I gotta go in, see what else Pa wants me to do this morning. I'm real sorry about your folks, Lew. Pa will give them a real good service."

"I'm sure he will, Percy. Go on. I'll see you at the funeral."

Percy left, and Lew listened to the voices raised in song.

It seemed to him they were singing out of tune, but it might have been just the way the sounds traveled through the walls of the church and then were carried away by the soft breeze that blew through the trees.

20

LEW SAW THREE RIDERS COMING DOWN THE HIGH ROAD INTO town. All of the farms around Osage had two roads leading past them, a high road and a low road. When the heavy rains came, only the high road was passable. The low roads were treacherous and dangerous. More than one buggy or horse had been washed away in floods.

As the riders drew closer, entering the town, Lew recognized them. He was surprised that all three were there, when he had expected only Bobby and Kevin. But Danny Slater was with them. All three carried shovels with them, tied on the back of their cantles. All were dressed in work clothes and boots. He stepped away from the hitch rail and unwrapped his reins. He mounted Ruben and rode toward them.

The three waved and Lew waved back.

He was glad to get away from the church and the singing. At least one of the singers was flat and the dissonance grated on his ears. Another went sharp on the high notes, and it was like someone grating chalk on a blackboard. The sound sent shivers up Lew's spine.

"Howdy, Lew," Bobby said. He was the oldest and the smartest of the three boys.

"Morning," Lew said. "Ready to ride out to the York cemetery?"

"That's what we come for," Bobby said. "Lord, what's the screeching?"

"Choir," Lew said.

The boys all laughed.

"Boy, we could use them in our cornfield come summer," Kevin said. "Make good scarecrows."

"Better at Halloween," Danny said.

Then the three sobered up as they saw how Lew was dressed. They all took off their hats.

"We're real sorry about your folks, Lew," Bobby said. "We don't like doing what we have to do."

"I know," Lew said. "Thanks."

The three young men fell in alongside Lew, and they rode toward the bridge that spanned the creek. Each adjusted his hat until it was just right on his head. All wore work gloves, Lew noticed. They were good boys. He and his brother David had grown up with them. Each had experienced tragedy in his family, he knew.

Bobby's baby sister, a little over a year old at the time, had fallen from her crib while her mother was out helping her husband with the haying. She had broken her neck, but one of their dogs dragged the dead baby out to the corn crib and mauled it pretty badly. The baby lay out there in the corn crib while the family looked for it, and rats had begun to eat away the little girl's face. When Bobby's mother saw what had happened to her daughter, she went half-insane. Bobby's father had killed the dog, burned the corn crib, and poisoned the rats, but his mother had never been the same since. She was a trifle addled, but every year, at the anniversary of her daughter's death, they had to tie the mother down because she tried to slash herself to pieces with a butcher knife.

As for Kevin, Lew felt particularly sorry for him. His father had been killed in a hunting accident, shot while calling turkeys in the woods. A hunter, who should have known better, let fly both barrels of his shotgun and blew Kevin's father's head almost off with No. 6 shot. That was bad enough, but Kevin's brother Tom was the one who had killed their father by accident. Tom had left home right after the funeral and none of the Smiths had heard from him since.

Danny's mother had been picking morels one spring and came home with two gunnysacks filled with mushrooms. Danny was at his granny's house over in Jasper at the time, with his father. His mother cooked up the mushrooms that night after inviting the neighbors over for supper. Some of the mushrooms were the poison kind. Danny's mother, along with a neighbor family and their two children, all died the next day. When Danny and his father got home, they found the bodies. Danny took a long time to get over the shock, and maybe, Lew thought, he wasn't over it yet. All three of his friends had dug a lot of graves, all right, some for kin of theirs.

None spoke on the ride to the graveyard, and when they tied up their horses in the woods and brought their shovels, Danny was the first to break the silence.

"This is about the prettiest graveyard around," he said. "'Specially in the fall." His curly blond locks tumbled from beneath his hat like tangled shavings from a wood plane.

"You're right, Danny," Kevin said. "I wouldn't mind being buried here myself." He didn't smile when he said it. Kevin almost never smiled and when he did, his teeth would just flash on and off like sunlight shining through trees in late afternoon when you glimpsed the woods from atop a running horse. Lew wondered if he was serious, or just obsessed by death.

The cemetery was enclosed in mesh fencing and there were sumacs growing all along the length of it. On a little knoll, the Yorks had planted maple trees. And, among the graves, there were redbuds and dogwood trees. In the spring, the cemetery seemed to light up with the white dogwood blossoms and the redbuds added a glowing crimson charm to the greenery. In the fall, the sumacs and maples were breathtakingly beautiful. The sumacs flared a bright red and the maple leaves turned to flame against the blue of the sky.

Lew walked to a spot between two dogwood trees spaced a dozen feet apart. The land was level there, rocky like the rest of the soil that hadn't been turned. He pointed to the center of the patch.

"Here's where I want to bury my ma and pa," Lew said. "Midway between these two dogwoods." They all glanced at a spot just to the left of the place where Lew was pointing. There was a grave there and a marble headstone with David Zane's name on it, along with the date of his birth and the date of his death. Beneath the statistics, there was a verse from some forgotten prayer.

"Our little angel has gone to heaven," it read, "where the Father loves him even more than we."

None of the young men mentioned David's grave, nor the untouched spot to the right of where the two new graves would be dug.

Danny laid his shovel down, walked back to his horse, and rummaged through one of his saddlebags. He returned with eight wooden stakes, a hammer, and a ball of twine wound around a stick. He took a tape measure from his pocket, nodded to Kevin, who took one end and ran it out until Danny held up his hand for him to stop. He drove a stake into the ground at one corner of one plot, then at the other. He measured sideways and drove a stake at the top. Then he and Kevin measured the other side and Danny marked the dimensions with another stake. He then ran the string around one stake and connected it to the others until he had a rectangle that measured three feet by six feet. He and Kevin then stepped off a small distance and did the same for the second plot.

"That look about right to you, Lew?" Danny asked.

"It does. Are you sure it's wide enough on both of them?"

"I think there'll be room to spare," Danny said.

Lew looked at the two string rectangles, then nodded. "Seems right," he said.

"All right. Let's dig," Danny said.

The three took off their shirts and picked up their shovels while Lew watched. They all worked on a single grave, Danny at the top, Kevin on one side, Bobby on the other side. Their shovels struck rock, and then all three would dig at the rock to loosen it, then one of them would remove it. They stacked the dirt to the far side of the grave, keeping the mounds loose and even.

"I hear Wiley Pope did that to your folks," Bobby said. "Him and that little peckerhead, Fritz Canby."

"That's right," Lew said.

"Both of those boys are no-accounts," Kevin said.

"Trash," Danny agreed.

"I'll bet the law ain't goin' to do nothing about them two neither," Bobby said.

"What makes you say that?" Lew asked.

"'Cause they sure as hell done it before, or just like it. And Wiley's old man paid off everybody so's they wouldn't press charges."

"Do you know that for sure, Bobby?" Lew asked.

"Hell, everybody knows about Virgil Pope and Luke Canby," Kevin said. "Wiley and Fritz can get away with murder and won't nobody do nothin' about it. That's for sure."

Lew felt his anger simmering just below the boiling point.

"Well, they aren't going to get away with this," Lew said.

"Oh?" Bobby said, stopping to wipe his forehead with a red bandanna he had tucked in his back pocket. The diggers were all sweating and their backs gleamed like the backs of wet seals in the sun. The first hole was taking shape, getting deeper and deeper. There was a pile of rocks stacked nearby, and that pile grew larger with each thrust of a shovel.

"They aren't going to get away with this," Lew said. "I don't care what their old men try to do."

Danny let out a sigh and stood up, leaning on his shovel.

"You be careful of those boys, Lew," he said.

"I'm not afraid of them," Lew said. "Or their pappies."

"Well, maybe you better be, Lew," Danny said, then resumed digging. "Them and their daddies are plumb mean and they don't give a hoot ner a holler for the law."

"Danny's plumb right about that," Kevin said. "Me'n Wiley got into it one day after school. I blacked his damned eye. Next day his daddy come by the house and told my daddy if I ever laid a hand on his boy again he'd find me at the bottom of a crick."

"Virgil told your daddy that?" Lew asked.

"He sure did. And he scared the living shit out of my old man. Kept me home for a week. After that, Wiley never let up on me and wasn't a thing I could do about it. If I didn't get killed by old Virgil Pope, my daddy would have given me a sound thrashing in back of the woodshed."

"Shit," Bobby said. "Them two, Fritz and Wiley, were the biggest bullies in school and if you was at a picnic or a pie social, them two would bring corn liquor and get all the boys drunk and steal their gals for themselves. They're rotten bastards."

The three young men were younger than Lew. They had been David's age when he died. So, Wiley and Fritz must have picked on the younger kids at school. Maybe even on his brother, David. Lew tried to remember them, but their paths hadn't crossed much. For some reason, Fritz and Wiley hadn't done anything to him and he just hadn't paid much attention to them when they were all in school together.

"You better be careful, Lew," Bobby said.

"About what?"

"If you got any notions of going after Wiley and Fritz by yourself, you'll run into a whipsaw with their pappies."

"Them too," Danny said. "Hell, they wouldn't think twice about shooting you plumb dead, Lew. I mean, those boys are born killers. Hell, they shot my dogs just for fun. Good coon hounds too. I guess we were all about ten or eleven at the time. They plumb enjoyed it."

"Well, look what they went and done to your folks, Lew," Bobby said. "Now, they didn't have no reason to hurt good people like your folks."

"No, they didn't," Lew said, the anger in him rising like the mercury in a thermometer on a hot day.

"Just you watch what you do about them boys," Danny said.

"I'm going to do something about them," Lew said. "You can count on it. They're not going to get away with what they did to my folks."

The three young men shook their heads. Danny knelt down and measured the depth of the first grave. He looked at Kevin and Bobby, and nodded.

Then they started on the second grave, digging along the lines of string that marked the rectangle.

Lew looked up at the sky, then over into the woods. He listened to the chink of the shovels as their blades struck pebbles and rocks, the swish of dirt as it flew through the air. Despite what his brother's friends had told him, he knew he was not going to give up, no matter what.

If it cost him his life, he was going to bring Wiley and Fritz to justice, see them both put in prison or hanged for the murders of his folks.

He kept his thoughts to himself, but they were murderous thoughts.

If the law didn't do its job, he vowed to himself, he would do the law's job.

No matter what it might cost him.

21

THE CHURCHYARD WAS CRAMMED WITH BUGGIES, WAGONS, carts, sulkies, and buckboards. Lew saw the milling crowd of black-garbed people and wondered where they had all come from. There were horses tied to hitch rails and posts, both in front and in back, and as he rode around the sea of people, he saw Skip Huckabee just driving his team away from the back door, his wagon empty.

Danny, Bobby, and Kevin had ridden home ahead of Lew to wash and put on suitable clothes for the funeral. Lew didn't know what time it was, but he knew the mourners had arrived early. The sun stood straight overhead and the church bells had not yet pealed. If not for the way people were dressed, it could have been a church social, Lew thought. People who had not seen each other all winter, or for a longer time, were laughing, talking, shaking hands, hugging.

Death, he thought, brings people together more than anything else in life. Death made a person conscious of his own mortality. Death was the uniting force among all peoples.

And why not, he said to himself. Death was the common denominator. It touched all peoples on earth. It was something that everyone understood, at least in one sense. No one understood the great mystery of death, but they understood that they were all subject to being touched by its icy hand.

He saw someone waving to him. Saw a hand really, above the crowd at the side of the building. He could not see who it was. Then the crowd parted as someone jostled people aside, forging a wedge through the throng. Lew stood up in the stirrups to see, but it was not until she emerged from a clutch of folks that Lew saw it was Seneca Jones. She saw him and she smiled.

He waved to her and stepped down out of the saddle to greet her as she came running up.

"I was beginning to worry when I couldn't find you," she said.

"Worry about me?"

"Yes, silly. I thought you might have forgotten, or . . ."

"Or what?"

"I don't know. Never mind. I'm glad to see you, Lew, although I'm sorry it's on such a sad occasion."

She looked beautiful, he thought. She wore a black dress with a lace bodice, lace cuffs on the long sleeves. Her hair was combed out and cascaded down her back like a silken black waterfall. She was one of the few women who did not wear a hat, and he was glad of that. Her face was radiant and her blue eyes shone like blue sapphires. Her high forehead emphasized the symmetry of her face with its patrician nose, full rouged lips, and delicately sculptured chin.

"You look very nice, Lew," she said. "All dressed up."

"You too."

There was an awkward silence for a moment as they looked at each other. The noise of the crowd wafted over them, but they were oblivious to all but each other. They were like two amateurs with foils, fencing, but afraid to touch the other. Lew tried to smile, but his lips were frozen in a doltish grimace.

"Oh," she said.

"What?"

"You want that paper I had Cletus sign."

She blurted it out as if it was the most important item on their minds at the moment.

"Uh, yes. Did Clete write down everything he saw the other day?" He shifted his weight from one foot to the other.

"I wrote it down. He signed what I wrote."

"Oh."

Another silence.

Then he looked at the purse in her hand. He hadn't noticed it before, despite its size. It was made of cloth and was black and had a brass fastener on it. That was all he could tell about it with such a quick glance.

"Did you bring it?" he asked.

"Yes. Do you want it now?"

He wondered if she wanted to hold onto it, dangling it as some kind of bait so that he would continue to be interested in her, interested in talking to her. It was an odd notion, but the thought crossed his mind like some fleeting incongruity that was of little consequence. Silly too, he thought, and was ashamed of himself.

"Uh, if you have it. I mean if it's not too much trouble."

"Are you going to tie up your horse, Lew? Or do you want him to read the document too?"

He was slow. He didn't understand her joke at first. When he did, he laughed.

"Yeah, I guess I forgot. I was going to tie Ruben up in back of the church."

"I'll walk with you," she said.

She made no move to open her purse, and that same thought rippled through Lew's mind again. Was she going to tease him over that eyewitness document? Make him beg for it?

The hitch rails were full, so he walked over to the trees at the foot of the ridge that rose up toward Possum Trot. He tied Ruben to a hickory tree. He heard Seneca open her purse. The hasp clicked. There was a rustle of paper. When he turned around, she held two sheets of paper in her hand.

"That it?"

She smiled and handed it to him.

"I hope it's what you wanted. Cletus didn't actually see . . . see what happened. Oh, Lew . . ."

He saw that she was still affected by the death of his parents. He could tell that she really hated to mention the gruesome murders.

"Don't worry," he said. "I'm just glad you got this from Cletus."

He read Sisco's account. The main point was that Cletus recognized Wiley Pope and Fritz Canby as the ones who were inside the store and that they came out with money and rode off toward Alpena. It seemed like solid evidence to Lew. The eyewitness had seen Wiley and Fritz run out of the store and when Cletus looked in, he saw what they had done to Lew's mother and father.

Lew's jawline tightened as he read the last of it. There was that anger, simmering inside him, threatening to boil over into a full-blown rage.

"I don't know if I did the right thing," she said.

"What do you mean?"

"I mean maybe I shouldn't have given you that document, Lew. Maybe I shouldn't even have talked to Cletus and asked him about what he saw."

"Why?"

She drew in a breath, held it for a moment, then let it out in a breathy sigh.

"I'm scared of what you might do with it."

"It's just evidence, Seneca. I mean to show it to Sheriff

Rudy Cooper over in Berryville, and maybe to Billy Jim Colfax, up in Alpena. I might even take it to Judge Wyman at the county seat, if Mike Farris, the county prosecutor, doesn't jump right on it and take action."

"Daddy and I were talking just last night about me giving you that paper today," she said. "He said I might just stir up a hornet's nest if I gave you Clete's statement."

"Ed said that? Why?"

"He had a run-in with Virgil Pope a few years ago."

"Seems like everybody's had some kind of trouble with that man."

"Virgil threatened to kill Daddy."

"What?"

"Daddy ordered lumber from Virgil at a certain grade and didn't get what he ordered. He wanted his money back or the right grade of lumber. Virgil refused. Told him, my daddy, that the grading was right and he wasn't going to get a refund or a different grade of lumber."

"That doesn't sound too serious," Lew said.

"Not at first maybe, but when Daddy said he was going to have Virgil arrested for fraud, it got very serious."

"Why, what happened?"

"Some men rode down in the nighttime and beat Daddy up. And just so he'd know who did it, they set fire to all that lumber and burned it right down to ashes."

"Did Ed report that to the law?"

Seneca shook her head.

"Why not?" Lew asked.

"He said that he got the message. He was afraid that the next thing to burn would be our home."

Lew felt the pressure in his teeth as he clamped them together as if trying to close off the rage he felt at this injustice. He wanted, just then, to lash out and strike someone, to smash Virgil Pope's face to a bloody pulp with both fists. With alarm, he realized that only violence could quell his terrible anger.

As if sensing the effect her story had on him, Seneca

touched his arm with her hand. She looked at him with a feeble smile on her face.

"That's all in the past, Lew. Forgotten. Don't get upset over something that just happened. Neither you nor I can do anything about it now."

"Maybe not, Seneca. But somebody has to teach Virgil Pope a lesson. People should not have to live in fear of that man."

"Please, not you, Lew. Let the law take care of Virgil Pope."

Lew snorted, but did not say anything. He drew a deep breath as if that would smother the towering fury that burned through his senses like a forest fire. He had seen one such fire, at night, when he was about eight years old, and had never forgotten it. It lit the sky with an eerie orange glow, and he could hear the snarl of the flames as they devoured trees and bushes, huge fiery tongues lashed by the wind that blew heat on his face and roared like a cyclone on the rampage. The next morning there was nothing left of the woods and the hill was bald and smoldering, with the smell of smoke in the air. He had never seen a more desolate sight and the images stayed with him, images that his anger had summoned up again after hearing what Pope had done to Seneca's father.

The first peal of the church bell broke through Lew's thoughts. The crowd suddenly hushed as the bell continued to ring, calling the people into the church for the funeral of Lew's parents.

"We'd better go in," she said. "Do you want me to sit with you? Reverend Cobb will want you to sit up front, in the first pew."

"Yes, please," he said.

"He told me if I saw you, to bring you in through the back door."

He held out his right arm and she slid hers inside, clasped his hand. They entered the church, and there was Harlan Cobb just inside the door.

"Lew," he said softly, his voice barely above a whisper, "would you want to say a few words before I deliver the final eulogy?"

"I don't know," Lew said.

"I thought you might like to talk about your ma and pa, give the folks some personal insights into their lives, tell the folks what they meant to you, and how much you miss them."

"I don't want to air my grief in public."

The church bells stopped pealing and Lew heard the rumble of footsteps as people filed in to the building, found places to sit.

"It would be a last farewell," Cobb said. "Nobody knew your parents better than you."

"Do it, Lew," Seneca said. "It will make you feel better and everyone here would cherish the memory of your words."

Lew saw the beseeching look in Seneca's eyes. He looked at Cobb, and the same expectant look was on his face.

"I might say something," Lew said. "Just a word or two."

Cobb smiled.

Seneca's face lit up and she squeezed his hand.

"Just go right on in," Cobb said. "An usher will show you two where to sit."

Lew walked through the vestibule with Seneca, out onto the stage, and down to the front pew, an usher pointing the way with a sweep of his hand. Lew saw the blurred faces of all the people looking at him. He felt dazed and disoriented, but Seneca guided him to their seats and he sat down with her, whispers floating through the church, wrapping themselves around him, blotting out the reason he was there.

And then, he saw the two caskets and something caught in his throat. He felt the tears well up in his eyes. They streamed down his face, and he was glad that the audience was at his back and could not see the sorrow that gripped him like a vise and shook him as he sat there, his throat aching with silent sobs.

22

THE CASKETS RESTED ON SAWHORSES TO ONE SIDE OF THE
stage. The supports were wrapped in black cloth; the caskets were draped with silk or taffeta, also black. Lew stared
at them, numb with grief, the blackness spreading to his
brain like some cloaking medication. The whispering died
down and the coughing and clearing of throats began as
Harlan stepped up to the pulpit and opened a book.

Seneca held Lew's hand and squeezed it once Cobb began to speak, reading a passage from the Bible. Lew heard
only a few of the words because he was thinking of his
mother and father lying inside those coffins, their bodies
filled with embalming fluids, their wounds powdered to no
avail, their outer flesh preserved, for a time, for some
hideous unknown reason. The entire process was ugly, he
thought, from the embalming to the funeral itself.

". . . have been taken away from us," Cobb was saying.
"Two of us will not be in this church tomorrow, O Lord, but
we know you hold them now in your kind and loving hands
and we pray that you have blessed them with your everlast-
ing light . . ."

Lew went deaf again as his thoughts drifted backward in time. Cobb had said much the same thing at David's funeral, and he remembered how hollow and meaningless they had sounded then. He concluded that Harlan was as ignorant of the great mystery of death as he was, as anybody was, and he found it hard to picture David riding on a white cloud up in heaven, plucking a harp and singing with the angels. Cobb, he decided, was making up a story for the living without any sure knowledge of what happened to a soul after death.

He heard the muttered and whispered amens after each telling point the preacher made, and he wanted to rise up, face the congregation, and shout at them. He wanted to tell them that the preacher was lying to them, because he had never been to that place called heaven. He hadn't died. He didn't know what death was, nor what lay beyond.

But Lew sat there and thought about Davey, and then he saw pictures of his mother and father when they were alive, and the preacher's words became a droning backdrop to the images Lew was seeing in his mind.

He saw his mother sitting by a winter fire, the flames dancing in the hearth, the wood crackling, shooting sparks up the chimney, sparks that danced like golden fireflies rising into the dark tunnel and floating into a dark sky. His mother had a dulcimer on her lap and she sang songs of planting and harvest, of rivers and oceans, and the sadness of losing a sweet child.

His father sat nearby, humming low in his throat, his chair creaking under his weight, while Lew and David sprawled on the floor like long-tailed cats with bellies full of milk, the music filling them, making their eyes leaden as they fought off sleep, and the wind howling outside, snow blowing against the windows like frozen moths beating their wings to get at the flame beyond the pane.

He felt his mother's hand stroking the hair at the back of his head as they all stood in the undertaker's place looking at the embalmed body of David. Mr. Goodwin had left them alone in the viewing room and it was so quiet, Lew could hear his own heart beating.

"It doesn't look like Davey," he had said to his mother.

"It isn't," she said. "David has gone to heaven. That's what he left behind, his poor body."

"But can he come back, Ma?"

"No, Lew. David can never come back. We have to remember him as he was."

"I don't understand why he had to die," Lew whispered.

"It was his time," his mother had said. "We each have our own time."

"It's not fair."

Later, at the funeral of his brother, Lew had rushed up to the casket and yelled at David's body.

"Davey, come back. Please don't go. Come back."

He would not do that now, Lew thought. He knew his parents were dead and gone.

". . . please turn to . . ." Cobb told the congregation the page number of the hymn, and Mrs. Kunkel began playing the opening chords of the song "Nearer My God to Thee," and Lew looked down at the hymnal in Seneca's hands, his eyes wet with tears, the words and the staff blurred and smudged.

And then Reverend Cobb was speaking again, extolling the virtues of Lew's parents, and Lew realized that Harlan had not known them, not known them at all. Cobb's remarks were so general, they might have fit any God-fearing Christian couple that he considered ideal members of his church.

Lew's thoughts drifted again, and Cobb's words sounded to Lew as if he were hearing them through balls of cotton stuffed in his ears.

He remembered the hunting trip he and his father had taken after David's death. Sam Huff had taken time off from the stave factory and gone with them. Sam had hunted in Colorado before and knew the way. Lew realized now that his father had taken him along so that he would stop grieving for his brother.

"He needs a change of scenery," his mother had said. "The trip with you, Del, will do the boy good."

Lew heard that and was reluctant to go because he thought his parents were trying to make him forget Davey. He didn't want to forget his brother and he became moody and withdrawn, refusing to talk to his father. He became belligerent and hostile toward both his father and Sam, and the farther they got from home, the more lonely he became. But at night, as the three of them camped under the stars, he would look up at the sky and he could feel his brother's presence. He began to think that David was with them, not in body, but in spirit, and that thought stayed with him during the long days that followed when they rode their horses across Oklahoma, into desolate Kansas, the prairie high with grass, antelope standing like statues, watching them as they passed, so far away he could barely see them.

Lew began to come out of his shell when they saw the buttes and mesas rise up like monuments on the land. As they traveled across the Great Plains, he was struck with wonder. As the land changed, so did he. He became awed by the immensity of the country, the hugeness of it, and the sky was even bigger. At night, he saw more stars than he had ever imagined were there, and often stood gape-mouthed at the sight of the Milky Way and the clarity of the constellations.

"You look a mite better today," Sam said one morning. "You been feelin' puny the whole trip."

"I wasn't feeling puny," Lew said.

"You wasn't yourself, son. Even your pa was growin' worry lines on his face."

"Well, I'm fine, Sam."

"Rarin' to go, are ye?"

"I'll go where you take us," Lew said with a sullen cast to his face.

"It's where you want to take yourself that matters, Lew."

"You mean, do I want to go back home?"

"I don't mean nothin'. You got to find your own meanin', boy. You can let life take you where it wants to, or you can take life with you and go your own way."

Lew thought about that now, as he sat there with a dazed look on his face, staring at the two caskets while Harlan rambled on and the restless audience showed its discomfort by shuffling its feet, clearing its throats, and inducing a series of fake coughs.

Sam had opened his eyes that day, but only a little. But Lew remembered that that was when he stopped thinking about himself and Davey and started noticing how his father and Sam conducted themselves on the trail. Both seemed comfortable in their own bodies and when they reached the end of the day, they were full of talk and good cheer. He found himself joining in with his own banter, remarking on the prairie chickens, the coyotes, the antelope he had seen. And when he saw buffalo for the first time, Sam and Del could hardly shut him up that night.

"Wait until you see your first elk," his father had said.

"Just a big deer, ain't it?" Lew said.

"Very big," Sam said. "And you're goin' to see muleys too."

"What are muleys?"

"Mule deer. They're big too, fatter than whitetails, maybe quicker. They live up high near where the snows are and they can run over rock slick as a mountain goat. And the Rockies have those too."

"Mountain goats?"

"Yep," Sam said. "And bighorns."

"Bighorns?"

"Bighorn sheep. They live high too, and climb straight on up a sheer cliff easy as pie."

"Oh, you're funnin' me now, Sam," Lew had said.

"No, he's not," his father said. "All those animals are in those mountains yonder."

"What mountains?" Lew had asked, looking out over the flat prairie.

"You'll see 'em by and by," Sam said. "Maybe tomorry."

Nothing had prepared Lew for the sight of the Rocky Mountains. When he saw them, he rubbed his eyes, thinking he was looking at one of those heat mirages such as they'd seen in Oklahoma and Kansas. But the closer they got, the more surprised he became, and when they rode up to the foothills, he saw the full majesty of the snowcapped peaks. By then, he realized he had nearly forgotten what home was like. It seemed to him he had been under those huge skies and under all those stars for all of his life.

They rode high into the mountains, so far back, Lew could see snowcapped mountain peaks wherever he looked. They crossed rivers and streams; they climbed rugged slopes and passes until the air was so thin he could hardly breathe. And when he saw his first bull elk, he had the worst case of buck fever he'd ever had. Its antlers had six points on both sides and when the elk swung its head, Lew thought it was the most beautiful animal he had ever seen.

They ate trout and mule deer, hunted elk in thick pine forests and in lush mountain meadows.

"You like it up here?" his father asked Lew one day.

"It's all right, I guess."

"We can go back home anytime you like."

"Do we have to?"

"Snows'll be coming soon. We leave now, we might get home for Christmas."

"I miss Ma."

"So do I. And I'm sure she misses us. One more day, and we'll leave."

He remembered how sad he was when they left the high country and started the long ride down to the plains. But it was a different kind of sadness, not like the sadness he felt now. It was as if he was leaving a home he had found and loved and to which he might never return.

Seneca shook Lew's arm.

"Lew, he said your name."

"Huh?"

"The reverend wants you to come up and say something."

Lew looked up. Harlan was beckoning toward him. Seneca put a hand on Lew's back and pushed him. He stood up.

"Go on," she said. "Everybody's looking."

Lew stumbled up the steps, and Cobb grabbed his sleeve and pulled him to the pulpit.

"Just say what's on your mind, son," Cobb said.

Lew saw the faces in the audience. They were all looking up at him, waiting for him to speak.

He took a deep breath and the fear left him. He looked down at the two caskets, then back toward the audience. He saw Seneca staring up at him. She looked to be proud of him, and he felt a tingling sensation all over his body, as if he had jumped naked into an icy stream high in the Rocky Mountains.

"There's no life there in those caskets," he said. "My folks have gone. They won't ever be back. But they're not dead."

The audience gasped.

"They're both alive to me and they always will be. My pa told me something once, when we were hunting elk up in Colorado. He said that life loves life. He loved life. And so did my ma. They both did. This life here was taken from them, but they'll find life wherever they've gone. That gives me comfort. They'll see my brother David and be with him again.

"My mother taught me to turn the other cheek," Lew said. "My father taught me 'an eye for an eye, a tooth for a tooth.' So, am I to forget how my folks died? Do I turn the other cheek?"

Lew heard a series of gasps that were like loud whispers, and he felt the preacher's gaze scalding the side of his face as if he had also gasped, releasing a gust of hot breath.

"If the law would work as it should," Lew continued, "then I could turn the other cheek. I could let justice take its course. But the two who murdered my parents, murdered them so brutally, have used up both of my cheeks. Two innocent, kind, loving, sweet people were beaten to death with the barrel of a pistol. It would have been more merciful to have shot them to death."

Another gasp from the audience. This one louder and more in unison than the other.

"I want that eye for an eye," Lew said, the level of his voice rising in intensity. "I want that tooth for a tooth. My mother gave me life. Hers was taken from her. My father gave me a home and his heart. His life was taken from him. They gave up their lives unwillingly, but I know they were both brave. And I know what they would want me to do. Justice should not have to wait until the Lord takes vengeance. Life loves life. Life fights against death, right up to the last breath.

"Well, I mean to exact vengeance upon those two murderers, Wiley Pope and Fritz Canby. For I believe in another axiom my father told me: 'He who lives by the gun shall die by the gun.' If the law won't hang those two men for what they did here in Osage, then I shall see to it that their days of living by the gun are over. They shall, by God, die by the gun.

"My gun, so help me, Almighty God."

Lew glanced out at the audience and saw that they all sat there in stunned silence, staring at him as if they couldn't believe what they were hearing.

"I thank you all for coming to say good-bye today," Lew said in a gentler voice. "It was a real nice service. We'll all of us cross that same river someday and come out on the other side. My ma and pa taught me that and that is what I believe."

He turned to the caskets, nodded at them, and then waved to the audience.

"I'll be seeing you," he said, and nobody there knew whether he was talking to the people in the congregation or to his parents lying dead in their caskets.

But many of them thought he was strange and that he had acted strangely in church.

Seneca took him in her arms when he descended from the stage, and she hugged him much longer than was proper under the circumstances.

But Lew was grateful. She was life and he embraced her, burying his nose in her hair and, as he had felt that day when they rode down from the mountains, he never wanted to let go or leave her.

The organ began playing and the choir sang "We Shall Gather at the River."

Seneca and Lew both began to weep in each other's arms.

23

VIRGIL POPE SAW THAT THE GATE WAS OPEN, AND MUTTERED A soft curse that he knew no one would hear. There was no reason for the gate to be closed. He had no stock on that land. But it was just the idea that Wiley would be so sloppy. The gate was there because it marked something Virgil owned. It set off his land, was a warning to trespassers to stay out.

He rode through it on the dappled gray horse he called Moondust. Moondust was eight years old and didn't move as fast he used to, but neither did Virgil. The horse was once a stallion, but Virgil had him gelded when he was three years old, taking all the fire out of his eyes. But he was still a good horse, and Virgil rode him as often as he could, which was not often enough. He rode him when he went deer hunting or bear hunting, and he rode him every Sunday morning while his wife traipsed off to church with the other old biddies of her sewing circle.

Virgil had not been to church in years, not since his parents had died in their burning house when they tried to save it from the Yankees who rode down from Missouri one drunken night demanding young girls. Union soldiers. Cavalry. Border patrol heathens. He hated the bastards for what they did that night, and he hated all Yankees and anybody who hailed from Missouri.

He rode up the road, looking down at the tracks that were still there, dusted over by the vagrant winds, the zephyrs that had died with the morning sun. Two sets of tracks. But he knew that was what he would find. His boy Wiley was thick with Luke's boy Fritzie, always had been. And he knew Wiley had gone up to that cave to hole up until after the talk died down about those folks down in Osage Wiley and Fritz had beaten up.

"We didn't know they was going to die, Pa," Wiley had told him. "We just had a little too much to drink and they was carryin' on so much, we hit 'em a little too hard."

Virgil knew his son was lying. Wiley had meant to kill those two old people. He had always been a wild one and he didn't mind spilling a little blood. If he had a few fingers of whiskey in him, Wiley was plumb bad. But Wiley was his son and Virgil would back him, help him out of trouble. Lord knows, he had done that often enough. And now, it looked like he was going to have to do it again.

He rode up the hill on the old wagon road, left it to climb another hill, then descended to the creek. He could see the cave up under the bluff above the creek, just barely, but he saw the hoof marks leading to the creek. He crossed it and climbed up the slope. The cave came into full view, its dark maw looming against the varied colors of the bluff.

"Wiley, get your ass out here," Virgil yelled. He reined up, let the horse sidle to a better position on the slope. He heard noises from inside the cave and a head appeared. It was Fritz.

"Mr. Pope," Fritz said, gawk-eyed as a fish out of water.

"Wiley in there?"

"Yes, sir." Fritz turned his head, yelled into the cave. "Wiley, your daddy's outside. You better get up."

"He still asleep?" Virgil said.

Fritz got to his feet, stepped outside of the cave. He yawned.

"We was up late, Mr. Pope. Then we went swimming and got plumb wore out. We was just taking a little nap."

"Don't you work for your daddy, Fritzie?"

"Not today. It's Saturday, sir."

"Well, Luke's sure workin'. I 'spect he could use some help."

"No, sir. He said he don't want me around."

Wiley crawled to the cave entrance and stood up, tucking a shirttail inside his trousers. His hair had dried and stuck out in all directions like darning needles in a huge pincushion.

"Daddy, what you doin' here?"

"I got to talk to you, sonny boy. You got your shoes on?"

Wiley looked down at his feet and shook his head.

"I'll ride up to the corral yonder. You and Fritzie come on up."

"Yes, sir," Wiley said, and vanished inside the cave. Fritz followed him.

Virgil clucked to Moondust and reined him in a tight circle. The horse clambered up the slope, dislodging dirt and rocks that tumbled down into the creek, making little plunking sounds as they struck the water.

Virgil dismounted at the corral and tied his reins to a post. He spread open his mackinaw coat and dug into the pocket of his overalls and pulled out a pack of ready-mades, Sweet Caporal. He filched out a cigarette, found a match, struck it, and lit the cigarette as he put the pack back in his pocket. He drew on the smoke and inhaled deeply. He looked around. The two horses inside the lean-to shed hadn't even whickered when he rode up. They were standing inside, hipshot, staring out with dreamy brown eyes as if they too had just awakened. Moondust switched his tail at a cloud of black gnats.

Fritz and Wiley topped the hill and ambled toward Virgil. Virgil thought they looked like a couple of schoolgirls skipping rope. He shook his head and puffed on his cigarette.

"What's goin' on, Daddy?" Wiley asked. "How come you to ride all the way up here on Moondust?"

"I think you got big trouble, sonny, that's why I rode up here. And I got better things to do."

"What trouble?"

"There was a funeral down to Alpena this evenin'," Virgil said. "For those folks you killed, the Zanes."

"Yeah? Fritz heard that in town yesterday," Wiley said.

"Well, I sent Billy Jim down there, just in case."

"Just in case what?"

"Just to see what folks were sayin', if there was any blood runnin' hot."

Virgil glared at the two young men. He blew smoke through his nostrils, which gave him a fearsome look. Fritz's eyes widened to the size of boiled quail eggs.

"Billy Jim went down to Alpena today?" Wiley said.

"He went to the funeral."

"I'll bet it was real nice," Wiley said with sarcasm.

"That son of Del Zane got up in the church and called out the names of both of you boys."

"He did what?" Wiley's face contorted in a look of high indignation.

"You heard me. Colfax said Lew Zane as much as said he was going to come after you boys and kill you."

"Let him come," Wiley said, an ominous tone in his voice. "I ain't afraid of Lew Zane."

"Billy Jim thinks Zane means business." Virgil said.

"People say a lot of stuff at funerals," Wiley said.

"Maybe so, Wiley, but you and Fritz better watch your p's and q's from now on. Billy Jim talked to the sheriff down there too."

"And what did the sheriff say?" Wiley said, a sneer on his face.

"His name's Swanson. Don Swanson and he said he didn't think Zane was going to give up on it. He said he'd told Zane to just forget about it, that the law wasn't going to do nothing, and Zane said he didn't give a tinker's damn. He means to come after you two with a gun."

"We got guns," Fritz said, his voice almost a squeak.

"Damned right," Wiley said.

"Well, just so's you know. I think you got a wildcat by the tail with that Zane boy."

"What about that witness?" Wiley asked. "Remember, you told me Billy Jim said Swanson had a witness."

"Oh, yeah, somebody named Sisco. Cletus Sisco."

"Yeah, that's the one."

"He's still a witness in case Zane does get somebody to bring you two to trial."

"And what if Sisco ain't around?" Wiley said.

"You better be careful, Wiley. You can't just go on killin' everybody around."

Wiley shaded his eyes from the sun and shifted his weight to one foot.

"We could beat up on Sisco," Wiley said. "Make him not so talkative."

"I think you boys ought to stay away from Alpena," Virgil said. "That seems to be a bad-luck place for you. Just lay low for a while. Zane will get over his temper and this will all be forgot."

Fritz nodded, eager to grasp at any straw.

"We are laying low," Wiley said.

"I don't need you at work, so just don't come around, hear?" Virgil said.

Wiley nodded. "Thanks, Daddy. Me'n Fritz will be all right. He don't have to go to work neither."

Virgil finished his cigarette. He dropped it onto the ground, heeled it into the dirt. He unwrapped the reins from the post and strung them on either side of Moondust's neck. He climbed up into the saddle, pulling on the horn to put his bulk into the saddle. The leather creaked under his weight.

"You boys got enough to eat up here?"

Both Fritz and Wiley nodded.

"You need anything, you let Fritz's ma know. I can get somebody to bring grub up to you. Don't be drinkin' no hard liquor neither."

"No, sir," Wiley said, trying not to smirk. Fritz had to suppress a giggle.

Virgil knew his admonition would have no effect on Wiley. The two boys reeked of whiskey and their eyes were puffy as if they had been bee-stung. But he had done the fatherly thing. And he had warned them about Lew Zane.

That was all he could do for now.

He rode back down the slope, crossed the creek, and left the gate open when he passed through it. No use closing it now, he thought.

Whatever had been done was done and too late to undo.

He would just have to wait and see what Lew Zane had in mind. If he came after Wiley, he just might get himself killed.

And maybe that would end it.

24

LEW THOUGHT IT WAS NEVER GOING TO END.

The house was filled with people, and the smell of food mingled with the aroma of cigar and cigarette smoke. Conversations threaded in and out of his ears, rising and falling with the randomness of ocean swells. He sat on the divan with Seneca nearby, but she was talking to Edna, who was serving the cake she had made that morning.

Lew had paid off Mr. Goodwin, fifty dollars for the embalming, another ten dollars for the caskets. He had also paid Danny, Bobby, and Kevin five dollars apiece for digging the graves and covering them up. They were surprised at the amount, saying two dollars was more than enough.

Twyman drifted by, talking to Ed Jones. Lew didn't know half the people who were there, but right after the funeral services, Edna had told him she was inviting folks over to help him make the "crossover."

"It's like a wake," she told him. "You don't have to be alone with your grief."

He almost told her that maybe he wanted to be alone with his grief. So many people came up to him afterward, patting him on the back, shaking his hand, that they all became blurred in his memory and he scarcely remembered any of their faces or identities. Seneca had saved him from some of it, leading him away from the throng of well-wishers, but then Edna had told him about holding the wake at his house, his parents' home. And he had been so bewildered by all the attention that he agreed.

He had seen a face at the funeral he had never expected to see. It startled him and worried him. Some of the people in the church had just streamed out, gotten into their carts and buggies, and left. Among them he saw Sheriff Billy Jim Colfax. Their eyes had met for a brief instant. Billy Jim had nodded to him, touched a finger to his hat in a silent salute, and then turned on his heel and walked to his horse. Lew thought that there was something ominous about that nod and that salute. As if the man expected to see him again, but not in a friendly way.

Lew shook his head when he was offered a plate with a piece of cake on it. He had eaten his fill of sausage, beef brisket, boiled potato, collard greens, and beets. Seneca too waved her hand to show that she didn't want any.

"Can I see where you sleep?" she asked.

"My room? It's not much."

"I just want to see it." There was a teasing note in her voice. He got off the divan and Seneca took his hand. He led her out of the front room and down the hall to his room. He opened the door and ushered her inside with a sweep of his arm.

"I tried to picture it in my mind," she said. "It's bigger than I expected. Bigger than my room at home."

"Is it?" He left the door open, but Seneca walked around him and pulled it closed.

His bed was against two walls at the back. A window looked out on the back garden and the well, the chicken house beyond, the rows of trees planted alongside a strawberry patch. Their leaves covered up the delicate plants every fall, and in spring, the berries pushed through and the green leaves found their way out of the mulch.

There was a handmade gun rack, with three rifles in it. One rack was empty, the top one. Next to it, on a peg, hung an old Navy Colt in .36 caliber jutting from a worn holster. There was a framed Currier & Ives hunting scene hanging on one wall, a small desk against the opposite wall. Seneca walked over to it.

"What do you use the desk for?" she asked.

There was a bookshelf on the wall above it and she looked at the titles.

"I sometimes write things down," he said, feeling suddenly exposed.

"What things?"

"Nothing much."

"Come on, Lew. Don't be shy. You can tell me. If you want it to be a secret, I'll keep it a secret."

"Just things I show, showed, my ma. Little stories. Poems."

"Poems?"

"Ditties really."

"I'd love to see them someday."

"Someday maybe."

"Do you keep a diary?" She turned and looked at him.

"No. I sometimes write things down in a ledger. I've got a bunch of them, from when I was a little kid."

"You always wrote in those ledgers?"

"I like to write," he said. "It relaxes me."

"I write sometimes too."

"You do?"

She smiled. "Yes. Private things. Thoughts. You know."

He laughed softly.

"Yeah, I guess I do," he said.

She turned away from the desk and came up to him. She put her arms around his waist.

"You've never kissed me, Lew."

"No, I reckon not. I don't like to take liberties."

"Do you want to kiss me?"

He drew in a breath. He felt dizzy. He nodded.

She tilted her head and squeezed him in her arms.

He looked down at her face, feeling giddy, lost.

Then he put his arms around her, pulled her to him. He kissed her on the lips, gently at first, then began to apply more pressure as she squirmed against him. He felt a surge of excitement as she pressed her body against his. Her arms left his waist and encircled his back. She tugged him still closer to her and her lips moved beneath his. The heat of her flowed into him, warming him all over, warming his loins. He felt as if he was falling from a great height, falling very slowly, floating. He closed his eyes and gave in to the feeling of weightlessness.

"Ummm," she intoned, and his giddiness increased.

He felt as if all the blood had drained out of his head. If he opened his eyes, he thought he might fall forward, as if he were standing on a high cliff and had lost his balance.

She rubbed her body against his, wanting him, and he knew she could feel the hardness of him because she rubbed against his manhood as if she wanted him to break through his trousers and enter her, rending the clothing that separated them.

There was a knock on the door and Lew broke his embrace. Seneca melted away from him.

"Seneca, you in there? Time to go on home."

"Yes, Daddy."

The door opened and Ed Jones stood there, looking at them. Seneca's hair was tousled. Lew glanced down at her and saw how ruddy her face was. Ed was God in the garden of Eden, glaring at them as if they were Adam and Eve standing there naked beneath the tree of knowledge, both good and evil.

But her father smiled at them.

"I got chores to do, hon," Ed said.

"I know, Daddy. I'll be right there."

"Lew, you can call any time."

"Thank you, sir. I-I'll do that."

The door closed and Ed's footsteps echoed down the hall. Neither had heard him come up, but now they heard him leave, as if he wanted them to know that he was not spying on them.

Seneca burst into giggles and Lew stood there, a sheepish look on his face.

"Seneca, I wonder what your father thinks," he said.

"You silly. He thinks we were kissing, that's all."

"Suppose he's mad?"

"No, not Daddy. But I'll bet he saw us leave the front room and come back here. And I'll bet he took out his watch and counted off the minutes before he walked back to this room."

"To check on you?"

"Yes. It's a good thing too." She looked serious then.

"Huh?"

She began patting her hair, straightening it. She had not worn pigtails that day, and her hair flowed like a black shawl over her shoulders, down her back.

"We might have gotten under the sheets together," she said, so matter-of-factly that Lew drew back, stared at her gimlet-eyed.

"What?"

"I wanted you too, Lew. You know that. And you wanted me. Didn't you?"

He had wanted her. He still wanted her. He wanted her to fill up the emptiness inside him, wanted her to hold him tight against her naked body as if he were a child and she his mother. Yes, he wanted her, and yet he felt guilty that he was thinking such thoughts on such a day. Such a sad day.

"Yes," he husked. "I wanted you, Seneca. I still do."

She stopped brushing her hair with her fingers. She stood on tiptoe and kissed him. He started to reach for her, but she danced away and started for the door.

"Come with me," she said. "I want to walk into the front room with you."

She baffled him. She acted as if nothing had happened between them. She seemed so lighthearted and not at all interested in his deeper feelings. It was as if she had been on a lark and was now skipping home, mindless as a schoolgirl. He followed her. She opened the door, took his hand in hers, and led him down the hallway.

Most of the people had gone, and more were leaving as if they had all heard some silent signal. Edna and Twyman were saying good-bye at the front door as the guests filed out. Ed stood in the middle of the room, his hat in his hand.

Seneca stopped suddenly and turned to Lew.

"What are you doing tomorrow?" she asked.

"I don't know."

"It's Sunday. Daddy and I will probably go to church. Why don't you come over in the afternoon? I'll make you supper."

He hadn't thought about what he would do the next day. On Monday, he planned to ride up to Alpena and show Sheriff Billy Jim Colfax the statement Seneca had gotten from Clete. Then he was going to find the man who made headstones and order two for his parents' graves. But Sunday? He had not thought of anything he wanted to do the next day except go to the graveyard and be by himself. Perhaps walk in the woods, sit by the pond.

"I don't know," he said.

"You don't have to come. I just thought you might like to."

"I want to. I want to see you again."

"Then come over. I'll be looking for you."

"All right. I will."

She smiled at him and walked over to her father. He put on his hat, nodded to Lew. They walked out. She waved at Lew as she went out the door, and she smiled. Her smile lingered on his mind for a long time after she left.

Lew mumbled to the last of the guests to leave, and then he sat down on the divan. Edna came up to him.

"Twy and I are goin' on home, Lew. I'll come back tomorrow and clean this mess up. I know you want to be by yourself."

"Thanks, Edna."

"Good-bye Lew," Twyman called from the kitchen. Lew heard the door open. Edna scurried away. He heard the door slam and then it was quiet. He looked around the room. There wasn't much to clean up. Edna had done most of that while the guests were still there, taking away plates and napkins, stacking them perhaps on the kitchen counter. Maybe that was the signal that told all the people to start leaving.

He got up and walked to the front window, looked out. He could see people down on the road, streaming back to Alpena. He saw Ed and Seneca in their buggy. He watched them until they disappeared. He looked out until the road was empty.

He bowed his head, suddenly overcome with emotion.

"Oh, Ma," he moaned. "I wish you were here."

And then, just when he thought he could not cry any more, the tears came once again.

25

LATER THAT SAME AFTERNOON, THE SKY BEGAN TO SCUD OVER with high cirrus clouds. Then the winds came, whipping and whirling, prowling like a sniffing wolf at the house, banging the shutters, rattling every loose board and fixture. The sky blacked with huge bulging thunderheads and the wind died down.

There was no sunset. Instead, Lew listened to the first patter of raindrops on the rooftop. The temperature dropped suddenly. Thunder boomed in the distance, and the night came on, bringing on the wind once again. The rain began to fall more heavily. The wind splashed it against the house until every window rattled. Lightning streaked the sky in lacy lattices so fleeting and intricate, they might have been illusions had not the thunder followed, roaring over the land like a billion angry lions all bellowing in unison.

The windows lit up with each flash of lightning, and the thunder rolled across the skies with a ferocious rumbling that seemed to make the earth shake beneath the shivering house. Lew had never heard louder thunder, nor seen more lightning, and the rains increased. When he looked out, he saw water running everywhere, tiny rivers squirming like silver snakes under the icy glare of the lightning strikes. He heard tree limbs crack and break, fall to the ground. He worried about the stock, hoping the cattle had found shelter, and was glad the horses were inside the barn.

He knew the creeks were already flooding and if the rain continued through the night, almost all of the roads would be impassable by morning. He had seen such flooding before, and lives had been lost in and around Osage and other communities. This storm was the worst Lew had ever seen.

He spent a restless night, sleeping fitfully as the thunder boomed and lightning flashed. Rains lashed the house with incredible fury. The thunder sounded like huge barrels rolling across a floor, the sound magnified a millionfold. Trees crashed around the house, uprooted by water and blown down by fierce winds that gusted to high velocities, making the house shudder.

Later, toward morning, Lew heard the hail smash into the walls of the house and pelt the windows like grapeshot. When he glanced out one of the windows, the ground was white, looking as if it were covered with mothballs. He shivered in the cold and lit a fire in the fireplace as the hail beat a steady tattoo on the shingled roof.

The hail stopped at dawn, but the rain continued to beat down. Lew looked up at the road leading to the bluffs and saw water running down through the mud. Debris lay everywhere, tree limbs, pieces of cedar needles attached to broken branches, rocks, dead rabbits smashed to death by the hail.

He knew he would not be able to ride to Possum Trot that day to see Seneca. Nor would Edna be coming over to wash dishes and help clean up the kitchen. The creek between Lew's house and the Butterfields' would be over its banks, treacherous. He was stuck there. The melting hail would add to the flooding, he knew, and it was not melting fast, despite the heavy rains.

The temperature outside was just below freezing, and the rain turned to sleet as Lew waded out to look at the thermometer and the rain gauge. The gauge was full at six inches. Both were nailed to a tree in back of the house, and the water came up to Lew's ankles. He went back inside and lit the stove. He boiled water and washed the dishes.

He spent the morning cleaning up everything, returning the kitchen to the neat state in which his mother had left it. He swept the hall and front room, dusted, ate lunch, napped in the afternoon. When he awoke, it was still raining and the wind was blowing the rain in sheets across the front field, blurring the barn and masking the lower pond, which had spilled over its banks.

Later, Lew put on waders and made his way to the barn. He had to lean into the wind on the way down and had trouble closing the front gate and the stock gate down at the barn. He wore a slicker that acted like a sail and made walking difficult. Through the slashing rain, Lew saw that the front doors of the barn were blocked by a thick batten of mud and debris. Rushing water had pushed every loose piece of lumber, tree limbs, and mud into a heap that pressed against the doors, making them impossible to open. He could barely hear the horses and mules inside as the wind howled and rain drummed on the tin roof, setting up a deafening din in the almost hollow building. He walked around the barn to the back doors, the rain stinging his face until it felt raw. These two doors were blocked by timbers he had cut and stacked the previous winter. Beneath the pile, water was running inside the barn, carrying with it copious amounts of silt and mud. The logs lay helter-skelter all along that end of the barn and were piled as high as his waist. It would take some time to clear them away. He knew the timbers were waterlogged and heavy. He had skidded them down from the ridge with the mule and had not yet cut them into small pieces. Each timber was probably too heavy for him to lift, much less move away from the doors without help from one of the mules.

Frustrated, Lew tugged on one of the top timbers. It did not budge. He heard Ruben whicker inside the barn and knew he was probably fetlock-deep in water, with no place to lie down that was dry.

"Damn," he said, and turned away from the storm-built dam, making his way back to the front, fighting the gusting wind all the way.

It took Lew an exhausting half hour to walk back to the house, as the wind shifted and blew into his face and pressed his slicker tight against his chest and legs. He passed the pond, which was still overflowing. There was a lake around the walls of the pond. The ground was saturated. It would hold no more water and he saw not a blade of grass in the field.

When the storm was over, he knew he would find arrowheads down in the pasture next to the creek where he had plowed the ground the week before it had snowed. They would be Osage arrowheads, chipped from the flint rock that could be found in abundance all around Osage and elsewhere. He knew something about the Osage because he had found traces of them on his property, along the creek, down at the Blue Hole. He felt pretty sure that the early settlers in Osage Valley had wiped out most of the tribe, and it saddened him to think of this travesty against human beings who had been born to the land. He would find arrowheads and put them in David's collection just as if he were still alive. He kept the box under his bed, along with other things Davey had owned: a quartz stone that glistened in the light like diamonds, a rattlesnake skin from a snake that Davey had killed when he was eight years old, a top that his brother had spun with a piece of waxed thread, a cracked geode he had found one day, a handmade set of wooden jacks, and a worn rubber ball, its surface full of gouges and scars, its red faded to a pale orange.

The rain continued throughout the night, Sunday, but the lightning and thunder ceased. And toward morning, the rain slackened until, by dawn on Monday morning, there was only a slow drizzle that gradually turned to mist as the sun tried to fight its way through the dark clouds.

Lew thought of Seneca and his broken promise. But she would know that the roads were awash and that there was no way he could ride up to Possum Trot. Even the high roads would be impassable, he knew, blocked at the bottom by tons of streaming water, new creeks and old, flooding every inch of land.

Lew arose early on Monday morning, haggard from lack of sleep, his eyes red-rimmed, small pouches of flesh bulging underneath as if he had aged overnight, or been on a week-long drunk. The drizzle had vanished, and he saw feeble sunlight through the window, small yellowish rays stabbing through the thinning clouds like lances fashioned of light. There was a fresh smell to the air, but there was also the stench of decay from the wormy and rotten tree trunks washed down from the ridges and hollows. The sight of these, lying strewn about, reminded him of the barn, its doors blocked, the stock inside probably hungry and thirsty.

Lew dressed in old work clothes, heavy, lace-up boots. He got a shovel from underneath the house and trudged down to the barn, sloshing and slogging over the sodden ground. The field was a small lake, the pond a forlorn island in the center, its muddy banks glistening dully in the sun.

The front doors looked to be the easiest to clear, and the barn slanted slightly that way. He began to move the heavier debris away from the pile of mud and leaves underneath. If he could get the front doors open, the water inside the barn would drain out and he could get to Ruben, saddle him up, and ride up to Alpena. There were no flooded creeks between his place and the Alpena road, and there were no creeks to cross on the way up. He wanted to take that statement of Cletus Sisco's to Sheriff Billy Jim Colfax and see if that would prod him to arrest Wiley and Fritz. He also wanted to see Virgil Pope if that didn't work.

Lew did not begrudge the work. Shoveling and sweating gave him time to think. He thought about all the obstacles he faced in bringing Wiley and Fritz to justice. It seemed to him that the right people, the judge, the sheriffs of three towns, were all against him. Those two killers were free and he was the prisoner. He was a prisoner of his own rage, a prisoner chained inside a dungeon, shackled, bound, victimized. Not only was justice blind, but the law in those parts was looking the other way. The judge, the sheriffs, all might as well have been blind. They were refusing to look at the crime and the evidence. Well, he would see to it that they did look at the evidence. If it was the last thing he did, he would see those murderers dead or in prison.

Lew felt all of these obstacles, these frustrations, building inside him just like the water that both filled the barn and had blocked him from entering it.

He dug and he shoveled and he wrestled the detritus stacked up in front of the barn. Sweat drenched his face and ran down his arms and legs. His clothes were wet and soggy as the sun climbed over the horizon and the light crawled across the meadow, shooting glints off the water that stood in the field.

He worked in anger. He worked as the rage inside him kept building, growing. Like the barn, he was filled with a substance that did not belong there and he had to get it out. There was nobody there to help him. Twyman could not cross the creek and come to his aid that morning. He was alone and the work was hard.

He cleared the last of the mud away from the doors and threw the shovel aside. He grabbed a door, pulled on it. He grunted from the effort, but the door gradually began to move. With a hard tug, he swung it open and water, shit, straw, dead mice, a snake, all flowed past him. He felt a sense of catharsis, of immense relief to see all those things rush out of the barn. He stepped to the other door and swung it open. More water and more dead things rushed to lower ground. The horses whickered. Pete, the mule, brayed and kicked the sides of its stall.

Lew sagged against the door as sunlight crept a foot or two inside the barn.

Ruben whinnied at him when he stepped inside, adjusting his eyes to the gloom. There was mud everywhere he looked, and there were more dead animals, swirls of straw, wet dirt swirled in watery shapes. But the water was almost all gone.

"Ruben," Lew said as he opened the stall door.

Ruben let out a low whicker.

Lew patted him on the neck.

"We're going to take a ride, boy," he said. "We're going to get us some justice."

The horse looked at him, switching its tail, silent as stone.

It lifted its head and looked toward the open doors, toward the sunlight, and it took a deep breath, blew it back out through its nostrils. Then Ruben bowed his head and bumped Lew twice on the chest.

"You big beggar," Lew said. "You want to go as bad as I do."

The horse bobbed its head as if it perfectly understood every word.

26

THE SHERIFF'S OFFICE IN ALPENA WAS CLOSED WHEN LEW rode up. There was a sign hanging on the door with a clock on it. The two hands showed the hour of 2:00. Below the clock it said CLOSED and above it BE BACK AT.

"Very clever," Lew said, and seeing a man sitting on a nearby bench, rode over to him and reined up.

"Know where the sheriff is?"

The man looked up at Lew and opened one eye. He had been asleep.

"He went over to Pope's Lumber. You just missed him. He should be back soon."

"Oh?"

"I'm here to take my brother back home. Billy Jim locked him up last night."

"And he wouldn't let him out before he left?"

The man shook his head. "Said my brother had to stay in the jailhouse until noon."

"What did your brother to do to get himself put in jail?"

"Peed on Billy Jim's dog yesterday."

"Why?"

"Why what?"

"Why did your brother pee on Billy Jim's dog?"

"He doesn't like that dog."

"Couldn't he have just paid a fine? Your brother, I mean?"

"He paid a fine. Billy Jim still locked him up."

"Billy Jim sounds like a fine upholder of the law," Lew said, a sharp sarcastic tone to his voice.

"Haw. That dog ought to be locked up. It bit my brother's wife a week ago. Billy Jim didn't do anything to the dog."

"Why not?"

"He said his dog doesn't like that woman. So my brother peed on it and he's in jail."

"Some kind of justice," Lew said.

"Billy Jim's justice."

"Thanks," Lew said, and rode off, shaking his head. The man on the bench stretched his legs, dipped his head, closed his eyes, and went back to sleep.

The main gate to the lumber yard was open and, beyond, Lew saw a log building with a sign on it that read POPE LUMBER COMPANY. He rode toward it, saw men loading planed lumber onto wagons out in the yard. He heard the sound of sawing coming from another building. There were hitch rails in front and along the sides of the office. One horse was tied to one rail, but Lew didn't recognize it. A rifle, a heavy Henry, jutted from a scabbard, and he guessed the horse must belong to the sheriff.

He dismounted and wrapped the bridle reins around an empty rail. He walked to the office door and opened it.

A young woman looked up from a desk. She had a ledger open and stacks of papers to the side of it. Wooden boxes held other papers. There were prints on the walls, but Lew didn't focus on them. The woman tried a smile, but it was obvious that she was absorbed in her work and resented being interrupted.

"Pick up?" she said.

"Huh?"

"Did you come to pick up a lumber order?"

"No. I came to see Mr. Pope."

"He's busy at the moment. May I tell him your name, sir?"

"Lew Zane."

Her expression changed. The color drained from her cheekbones and her mouth went slack. Light danced in her eyes as she raised her head and caught the sunlight spraying through the window like a golden mist.

"Something the matter?" Lew asked. Her fingers were undulating atop the ledger as if she were searching for the pencil that had dropped to the side.

"Uh, no, I mean . . ." As if her mind had gone blank, she closed her mouth. She rose from her chair. "Be right back," she said, and the phrase was all one word run together.

She walked back to a door and opened it. Lew looked at it. VIRGIL POPE, PROP. was painted in block letters at eye level. The door closed as the girl disappeared. Lew heard voices, hers and a man's. Then he heard another voice, one that he recognized. Billy Jim Colfax was inside the office with Pope. Lew tapped his chest and heard the papers in his pocket make a crackling sound.

The young woman came back into the room, closing the door behind her. The voices died down, but Lew could still hear their murmur.

"You can go in there if you want," the woman said, her face slightly ashen. "But . . ."

"But what?" Lew looked at her more closely, studying her face for signs of recognition. She appeared to be in her midtwenties. She wore a sweater over her plain cotton dress, which was dyed a pale green. Her cheeks were lightly rouged, as were her lips, and her hair framed her face in comely ringlets. She had hazel eyes that flashed gold, brown, and blue-green.

"I think Mr. Pope and Sheriff Colfax are mad at you, Lew."

"Do I know you?"

"I used to see you at school. Here in Alpena. You were three or four grades behind me."

"I don't remember you. I'm sorry."

"I'm Paula Rose. I mean I am now. I married Bill Rose."

"Sure. I remember Bill. And you were his gal in school."

She blushed.

"That's right." She leaned over and spoke in a whisper. "Mr. Pope's in a bad mood," she said. "And I think Sheriff Colfax is too."

"I'm going in. Thanks, Paula." He walked past her desk and opened the door behind her.

Lew stepped into a windowed room that afforded a view of the lumberyard. The office smelled of pipe tobacco and wood shavings. But there was no sawdust on the floor. Seated behind the desk was a man in overalls, and to one side, in another chair, sat Sheriff Colfax.

"Have a seat, Zane," Virgil Pope said, leaning back in his chair. "I reckon you come to see me about something. You know Billy Jim."

"Yes," Lew said, and sat down.

"What's on your mind, son?" Pope said.

"You might not want to hear it, sir."

Pope laughed. Colfax looked at Lew with cold hard eyes just barely visible behind narrow slits.

"You go right ahead, Zane. I'm all ears."

"I came up here to file formal criminal charges against your son Wiley, Mr. Pope. Against Wiley and Fritz Canby. They brutally murdered my folks and robbed them. There is a witness to the crime."

Pope's expression changed. His jowls hardened and his lips compressed so tightly they almost disappeared. His demeanor shifted from affability to hostility. All in an instant.

"You listen to me, sonny. You file them charges and you'll regret it the rest of your life."

"I'm filing them."

"Wiley's a good boy," Pope said. "Him and his friend Fritz got a little drunk that night, the way I hear it. Wiley just likes a little excitement now and then. I understand your folks got robbed of forty dollars." Pope reached into his pocket, pulled out a roll of bills. He peeled off four ten-dollar bills, put them on the desk, and shoved them toward Lew. "Here. That should take care of that. There's your money back, what was stole, you say, from your folks. And I'll even pay for the funeral. What did it cost? Fifty dollars? Here." Pope counted out five more ten-dollar bills and added them to the stack. The bills lay there between the two men. Lew made no move to pick up the money.

"Money won't replace the lives of my folks, Mr. Pope," Lew said. "Your son and Fritz are going to pay, though. They're the ones who owe me two lives. You can't buy them out of this. Your son's going to pay this debt. Law or no law."

Lew looked over at Colfax and said the last phrase again.

"Law or no law, Mr. Pope."

"Meaning what?" Pope said.

"Meaning, I mean to bring Wiley and Fritz to justice myself if Billy Jim won't arrest them."

Colfax just glared at Lew. He didn't say a word.

"Zane, if you touch a hair of my son's head, I'll kill you myself." Pope's eyes flashed as they widened.

"Did you hear him threaten me, Billy Jim?" Lew said to the sheriff.

"It's Sheriff Colfax to you, Zane. And I didn't hear no such thing."

Lew got up.

"All right," he said. "You've made your choice, Mr. Pope. And if Colfax backs you, then I have to make a choice. Wiley's going to pay for what he did."

"You better heed my advice, Zane," Pope said. "You try and take the law into your own hands, you'll be mighty sorry."

"What law, Mr. Pope?"

Lew walked out of the office and slammed the door behind him.

Paula looked up at him, but he swept on past her and out the front door.

Lew heard pounding footsteps as he reached for his reins. He turned toward the office and saw the door burst open.

Billy Jim leaped past the steps and landed on the ground. He drew his pistol.

"Hold on there, Zane."

Lew froze.

"What in hell are you doing, Billy Jim?"

"I'm arresting you, Zane. Don't you make a damn move or I'll blow a hole in you right where you stand."

Colfax shoved the snout of his pistol into Lew's gut. He cocked the hammer. He reached down and jerked Lew's pistol from its holster, shoved it inside his belt at the waist.

Lew felt a clammy hand at his throat. Fear gripped him as he faced death a mere heartbeat away.

"I ought to shoot you," Colfax said. "It would sure as hell solve a lot of problems."

Lew heard a noise on the porch of the office. He looked past Colfax and saw Virgil standing there, his hands in his pockets. The man had a smile on his face.

"I'll come down and sign the papers, Billy Jim," Pope said. "Maybe that boy will cool off after a night or two in your jail."

"Come on down anytime, Virg," Colfax said.

Pope walked back into his office, a smirk on his face.

"Turn around, Zane, and climb on your horse. I'll be right behind you. If you run, I'll shoot you down like a damned rabbit, you hear?"

Lew grimaced in rage.

He unwrapped the reins and climbed onto Ruben. Colfax walked to his horse. In moments, they were riding out of the lumberyard, heading for the jail.

Colfax rode up alongside Lew.

"You know, Zane, I tried to warn you to forget about what happened down in Alpena the other day. Nobody gives a damn about you or your folks. You're messing in something that's just too big for you to handle."

"I guess a man like Virgil Pope can buy a sheriff just like I can buy an old mule."

"You just keep your mouth shut, Zane. You're in enough trouble as it is."

"What are you charging me with, Billy Jim?"

"Threatening."

"Threatening?"

"I heard you tell Virgil you was going to kill his boy."

"I never said that."

The man was still sitting on the bench near the sheriff's office. Waiting. He woke up as they passed and got to his feet.

"My word against yours, Zane," Colfax said.

Lew seethed with anger. If this was the way the law worked, he wanted no part of it. Justice in the Ozarks might be as blind as anywhere else. But it played favorites in this part of the country. And men like Colfax and Pope were the ones balancing her scales.

27

FRITZ BLEW ON HIS CUPPED HANDS TO WARM THEM. HE SHIVered in the predawn cold, even though he wore a heavy woolen coat. His fingertips were still numb from being in the water of the creek.

"Stop shivering, Fritz," Wiley whispered. "You make too much noise."

"I-I'm c-c-cold."

"You look like a dog shitting peach seeds."

They both laughed, but the laughter sounded like heavy puffs of air. They were trying to be quiet. On the other side of the road a whippoorwill trilled the same monotonous phrase they had been listening to for the past fifteen minutes.

The sun was just starting to come up. In the east, a rip in the sky, with pale cream pouring out. Just enough light for the two to see each other squatting in thick brush near the creek just north of Osage.

"He ought to be coming up thisaway pretty soon," Wiley said.

"What if he don't?"

"You peckerhead. You checked that trap, right?"

"Yeah, I checked it. Froze my fingers to the bone too."

"And they was a muskrat in it, right?"

"Yeah, Wiley. There was a drowned muskrat in the damned trap."

They had left their horses tied and concealed some two miles upstream and walked along the trapline. This was the first trap that was tripped and filled. There was a lot of stumbling and falling to get to this place, but they were here, waiting.

"Took long enough for this creek to go down," Wiley said. "It's still running pretty full."

"It's running damned cold too."

The two had spent nearly a week scouting the creek, watching Sisco check the water level each day and finally set his traps. The day before, they waited in vain because Cletus didn't check the trapline. They spent a cold night camped in the woods. They talked and they planned. They grew excited about what they were going to do.

"By the time Zane gets out of jail," Wiley said, "he ain't goin' to have no witness to nothing."

"Yeah. We can thank your pa for that. And the judge. Shoulda given him more'n thirty days, though."

"It'll teach Lew Zane a lesson," Wiley said.

"He oughta be tarred and feathered." Fritz suppressed a giggle. "Wouldn't that be somethin'?"

"Shhh," Wiley said. "I think I hear somethin'."

They did hear something. Someone was walking along the creek bank on the opposite side from where they squatted. They could hear the crunch of boots on stone and sticks, the mushy squash as a boot stepped into mud and water, the soft sucking sound as the walker pulled his boot free of the quagmire. The whippoorwill's cry cut off midsentence as if a door had slammed shut on it. In the ensuing silence, the squish, plop, thud, splash of boots on the soggy ground.

"There he is," Fritz whispered. "I see him."

Wiley saw the dim shape of a man walking toward them. In the dim light, the man looked like a troll. He was carrying something limp and it slapped against his leg. Wiley squinted. It looked like an empty gunnysack, but he couldn't tell for sure. But there was no clank of traps, so whoever was coming had not checked the line below them. Wiley had thought that the trapline started where they were. They had not gone any farther than this. They had walked along the creek with a stick in the water. When the stick struck something soft and yielding, Wiley had made Fritz put his hands in the water to see if there was a muskrat caught in a trap. And Fritz had done that.

"He's a-comin' right to it," Fritz whispered.

"Shhh." Wiley breathed heavily. He drew his pistol. Fritz saw this and reached for his own pistol. He slipped it from its holster and winced when his fingers touched the cold metal that separated the grips on the butt.

"Is it Sisco?" Fritz leaned close to Wiley's ear and his whisper was soft as spider silk.

Wiley nodded, leaned forward a little to see past a branch of the bush next to him.

The pale pastel of the eggshell sky to the east spread higher and wider. Streaks of golden light began to sizzle on the horizon like fired tongs pulled from a blacksmith's forge. Gold and red splayed into the ether and the last star faded out. The moon paled to a mere outline scrawled against the cobalt sky.

Sisco walked to the sunken trap. He dropped the empty gunnysack onto the ground. He picked up a stick and poked it down into the water. He prodded and when he felt the dead muskrat, he stood up, dropped the stick, and stepped across the creek. His stride was too short and his boot plunged into the water. He let out a *whoo* sound and put the other foot in, then stepped up onto the bank nearest Wiley and Fritz.

"Now?" Fritz whispered.

"Wait." Wiley's eyes gleamed. He licked his lips as a cat reacts to food.

Sisco reached down and pulled up the trap. He opened the jaws and released the dead muskrat. He held it up to the light.

Wiley stood up. He cocked his pistol and Sisco whirled around.

Fritz got to his feet. He also thumbed back the hammer on his Remington .36-caliber converted New Army.

"You got a big mouth, Sisco," Wiley said.

Sisco saw the pistols. From his expression, he recognized Wiley and Fritz.

"Oh, shit," Sisco said. He dropped the trap. The chain jangled as it struck the ground. The muskrat left his hand as well.

Then Sisco whirled away from the two young men and dashed back across the creek, splashing water from his pounding boots.

Wiley took aim and fired his pistol.

Fritz started shooting.

Lead ripped into Sisco's body. He writhed in a macabre dance as bullets struck his arms and legs, his back. He turned, and the two men kept firing until their pistols were empty.

"Go get the horses, Fritz," Wiley said, his voice dead calm, steady.

"I want to see what we done to Sisco," Fritz whined.

"Better reload your hogleg case somebody heard them shots and comes here to see what for."

Wiley crossed the creek, flipping the cylinder gate open and ejecting the hulls of his bullets into the stream, pushing the rod as he spun the cylinder. As he approached the fallen Sisco, he shoved cartridges into the cylinder until all six were filled. He closed the gate and cocked the hammer back.

"What about you, Sisco? You got any breath left in you?"

Fritz came up and stared gape-mouthed at the body of the man on the ground. Sisco's clothes were splotched with blood. His coat was torn and frayed where the bullets had entered. He was not moving. He did not appear to be breathing.

"I think he's plumb dead, Wiley," Fritz said in a breathy whisper.

Wiley kicked Sisco in the side. Sisco didn't respond. He kicked him again, harder, just to make sure.

"If he was alive, he'd howl," Wiley said.

"Then he's dead, ain't he, Wiley?"

"He won't flap his tongue in no court," Wiley said. "Now, go get the damned horses. We got to get the hell out of here."

Fritz shoved his pistol in its holster and took off running. He leaped the creek at a narrow point and kept on running like a man scared of his own shadow.

Wiley smiled.

"You don't have to worry no more, Daddy," he said to himself. "There ain't no witness to nothing."

Wiley started walking toward the creek. The sun began to leak light through the trees beyond the creek. He couldn't even see Osage from where he was, and there was nobody coming to investigate. Cletus Sisco was dead and Wiley didn't have a worry in the world.

He sniffed and drew breath. He smelled the sweetness of the morning and it was like an elixir. He felt good. Damned good.

28

BACON, BEANS, AND CORNBREAD. THE CORNBREAD WAS ALIVE with weevils. The fatback bacon was tough and stringy. The beans were always stale and hard as marbles. The food was the same every day. And every day, a little wizened lady named June Bug Timmons brought the meals in a wicker basket covered with a red-and-white checkered towel.

Billy Jim unlocked the cell door and stood there, a hand on his pistol while June Bug waddled in, set the basket on the floor, hoisted the towel with a flourish, and set the pewter plates on a little square stool. Then she left the basket, took the towel with her, and said she'd be back for the dishes in a half an hour. Morning, noon, and night.

"Do you cook this shit or shovel it out of a stall down to the stables?" Willie Cushman asked as June Bug stood up and flashed her carious smile with its broken and blackened teeth.

"You watch your mouth, Cushman," Billy Jim said.

"I does the best I can with what I'm given," June Bug said with an indignant air. "The county don't pay but next to nothin' and I cooks what they brings me."

"My dog eats better'n this," Willie said.

June Bug pranced out of the cell. Billy Jim slammed the door shut and turned the key in the lock.

"Your dog probably ain't no criminal, Willie."

Willie, a dour-faced man in his forties with streaks of gray in his thinning hair, cast a jaundiced eye on Colfax and cocked one eyebrow.

"You wouldn't know a criminal if one came up and bit you on the balls, Colfax," Willie said.

Colfax glowered, then marched down the hall. A moment later, Lew heard the door slam and then the clatter of a key in the lock. He sat on the edge of the bunk. Willie handed him a tray. They had tin cups and a pitcher of water that was filled once a day. Willie poured water in his cup, then looked at Lew. Lew held out his cup and Willie poured it half full, the same as his. There were no eating utensils, so the two ate with their hands.

"Everything to humiliate a man," Willie said as he scooped up some beans.

"If you feel that way," Lew said.

"What do you mean? Don't you feel degraded having to gobble food down like an animal?"

Lew shook his head. "Nope. A man like Colfax can't make you feel anything you don't want to. It's food, and I'm grateful for it. I'm sure humans ate food this same way a long time ago before someone invented knives and forks and spoons."

"Yeah, cavemen maybe."

"Watch out for rocks in the beans," Lew said. "I near broke off a tooth last night at supper."

"Was it a round rock or a square one?" Willie said.

Lew laughed. "I think the one I chomped on last night was shaped like a pyramid. Kind of triangular."

"Yeah, well, those are the easy ones to detect. It's those little round bastards that drive me plumb crazy."

Willie was arrested and brought to jail because he stole a loaf of bread from the grocer in Alpena. He was Lew's third cell mate since he had been incarcerated, and the most interesting. At the time Willie stole the bread, he hadn't eaten in a week and he had no money. He told Lew that he had offered to work for food, but everyone he had asked had turned him down. His hunger had done something to him. He ate now like some ravenous beast, shoveling food into his mouth with his fingers, chewing it up and breathing heavily.

"You don't talk much about yourself, Lew," Willie said as he sopped up the bean juice with the last of his cornbread. "And I don't know why Colfax won't let you have any visitors."

Lew was angry about that. He knew that Seneca had come up to see him, but Colfax had refused her plea to visit him. Twyman had also come to visit, but was not allowed to see or talk to Lew. Colfax made sure that Lew knew about these visitors who had been turned away.

"I'm being punished," Lew said.

"Isn't jail punishment enough?"

"Not to Billy Jim. Not to Virgil Pope. Or Luke Canby, for that matter."

"Well, it ain't right," Willie said.

"My day will come," Lew said.

"What do you mean?"

"I can't talk about it. That's what got me in here in the first place."

"You mean threatening Virgil Pope."

"I'm the burr under his saddle, I reckon."

"I guess so." Willie dropped his plate on the floor. It clattered as it rocked and finally settled. Lew set his own plate down. His stomach was already hurting from the bad food. He drank water from his cup and stood up, stretching.

"At least you get to get out of this cell, Willie."

"Yeah. The judge sentenced me to hard labor. I'm paying for the loaf of bread I stole, even though the grocer got it back."

Every morning, Colfax took Willie out of the cell and

took him down to the grocery store, where he swept up, re-stocked the shelves, lifted heavy bags. Billy Jim brought him back at noon in time for the meal they just finished.

"Six months seems a long sentence," Lew said.

"Colfax said he probably could have hanged me for what I did. He said that if I had run, the grocer could have shot me dead and nobody would have cared a whit."

"Willie, if you're looking for justice here in Carroll County, you won't ever find it."

Willie started to say something, but they both heard the rattle of a key in the lock of the office door. The door squeaked open and Colfax appeared.

"You got a visitor, Zane," the sheriff said. "This one gets to talk you."

"Who is it?"

"Someone who's got some news for you, Lew."

"Good news, I hope."

Colfax laughed. A moment later, he opened the door wider and Sheriff Don Swanson walked through. Lew's heart plummeted as if it had fallen through a trapdoor in his chest.

Billy Jim closed the door behind Swanson, which surprised Lew. Whenever Willie had a visitor, his brother, an uncle, his mother, Colfax always stood next to the person and listened to every word exchanged between visitor and prisoner.

"Swannie," Lew said. "I'm surprised to see you here."

"Well, I had to come by. I'm on my way to Berryville to report a crime."

"What does that have to do with me?" Lew walked over to the bars and stood in front of Swanson.

"Your witness died this morning."

"My witness?"

"Cletus Sisco. He's dead."

Lew's mind went vacant. He stared at Swanson while he felt an invisible knife twist in his gut.

"You said a crime. Did Clete not die of natural causes?"

"He was shot to death."

Lew sucked in a breath, let it out through his nostrils. He felt dizzy, disoriented.

"Somebody shot Clete?" He knew the question sounded stupid, but Lew was trying to digest the scant information and make it fit into everything else that had happened to him.

"Shot him to pieces."

"Do you know who did it?"

Swanson shook his head.

"Nobody saw it. Clete was working his trapline. Could have been anybody."

"No, it wasn't just anybody, Don. You know damned well who killed Clete. Or had him killed."

"Now, don't you go off half-cocked, Lew. You start making accusations, you'll just get yourself in more trouble. When I go over to Berryville, I'm going to talk to the judge and see if he won't turn you loose. A lot of people got together down in Osage and made up a petition. They charged me with delivering it to Judge Wyman."

"A petition?"

"Ed Jones and his daughter started it up. Sam Huff got everyone at the mill to sign it. Seneca rode around. Nigh everybody in Osage wants you back home."

"What about you?"

"It don't make me no never-mind, Lew. I just want you to forget about making a case for murder. Your only witness is dead, and so is the investigation into the death of your folks."

Lew didn't say anything. Swanson too just wanted him to forget about the murders and go back home and be a good boy.

"Thanks for telling me, Swannie. Do you think the judge will let me out before my thirty days is up?"

"I talked to Virgil Pope before I come over and he's willing to let you go. All he wanted was for his son to be left alone. You take my advice, you'll do just that."

Lew's jaw tightened as he ground his teeth together.

"All right," he said.

"You mean you'll mind your own business and leave the law to do its job?" Swanson asked.

"Yeah, Don."

"I'll tell the judge that. Good luck."

Swanson walked out and both Willie and Lew heard Colfax lock the door again.

"So, Lew, it looks like you'll be going home maybe."

"Maybe."

"You don't sound too happy about it."

"The law here is sweeping everything under the rug. My folks were murdered by two worthless criminals and the law is not going to do a thing about it."

"You know something, Lew?" Willie said. "My pap told me a long time ago, and he heard it from his pap, who come out here in '38 from Tennessee, that when a man comes to a town with no law, he's got to show some gumption."

"What do you mean?" Lew asked.

"I mean, when there is no law, you got to be the law."

"Like a vigilante," Lew said.

"Yeah, kinda like a vigilante. When my grandpap run into a bully takin' over a town, he went to the marshal, who told him to mind his own business. So Grandpap called the bully out and shot him dead."

"What did the marshal do?"

"When the marshal come after Grandpap, why, he shot him dead too. He became the law right then and there. And nobody said a damned word."

"I wish your grandpap was the law here in Carroll County," Lew said.

"Well, he ain't. And you've had a taste of the law here."

"Lawlessness, you mean."

Willie smiled. "Well, there's your answer, Lew. Maybe you've got to become the law. Maybe you are the law."

Lew sighed, his mind racing like a horse running free in the wind.

I've got to become the law, he thought.

And the pain of the knife twisting in his stomach went away.

Cletus Sisco, his only eyewitness to the murder of his folks, was dead. But Lew still had his account of the murders on paper. But would the law accept that and bring two murderers to justice?

If not, then he would.

He would become the law.

29

EDNA BUTTERFIELD STOOD IN THE STOREROOM AND COUNTED out the day's receipts, separating the bills and coins by denominations until they were each in neat stacks and piles. She used Jenny Zane's abacus to tally the daily totals, then entered them in the same ledger Jenny had used. She put the money in the same strongbox that had been emptied the day of Jenny's and Del's deaths. She put the ledger on a different shelf, however, not in the storeroom, but in the store itself, behind and underneath some bolts of colored cloth. And she didn't leave the strongbox in the storeroom where Jenny had kept it, but put it in a hatbox and waited for Twyman to pick her up in the buggy and take her home.

"About finished, Edna?" Seneca asked as she entered the room. "I finished sweeping up and put everything away."

"Yes, I'm done. You can go on home now, Seneca. The end of a busy day."

Seneca brushed away a strand of hair that had fallen over her cheek.

"You look tired, Edna. And worried."

"I am tired. And worried. But Lew will be back home to-morrow and I can give him all the store money. I don't feel right about keeping it all at home. It makes me nervous."

"Where else could you keep it?"

"I don't know. No place, I reckon."

"There's something else, isn't there?" Seneca asked.

Edna closed the lid on the strongbox. She reached up for the hatbox on the shelf. She brought it down, set it beside the money box.

"I don't know, Seneca. I feel like I'm . . ."

"Like you're what?"

"Like I'm being spied on at night. When Twy comes to take me home."

"Is someone following you, you mean?"

Edna lifted the top off the hatbox and put the strongbox inside. She put the top back on and sighed.

"I don't know. Them woods around us, and along the road when Twyman drives us home. I think I see somebody in them, but when I look, there ain't nobody."

"Maybe it's just your imagination. Knowing what happened to Jenny and Del."

"Maybe. That's what Twy says anyways."

"So, you've told him about your feelings?"

"He don't like to hear me talk about 'em."

Seneca walked over and patted the back of Edna's hand. She had been helping Edna ever since Lew was put in jail. They had become even stronger friends.

"Don't you worry. Twy will take care of you. And as you said, Lew will be home tomorrow. That was good news Sheriff Swanson brought us this afternoon."

"I keep thinking of poor Cletus," Edna said. "And the Zanes. What happened to all of them? Would you lock the back door for me, Seneca? I'll wait in the front for Twy."

"Sure, Edna. I won't go home yet. I'll wait with you."

Edna picked up the hatbox, carried it out of the storeroom, and walked toward the front window. Seneca opened the back door for a brief moment, then swung it shut.

Something caught her eye before it closed. She wasn't sure what it was. A glint of light in the woods to the left of the church graveyard. A piece of metal caught by the sun? A mirror? She pushed the door open a slight crack and looked in the direction where she had caught the fleeting flash of light.

She saw nothing.

She closed the door, locked it. Then she walked out into the store, saw Edna standing in front of the window looking out. She glanced at the counters and shelves as if to make sure she had put everything away.

"He's late today," Edna said.

"Oh, you know. He was working that ditch at Lew's, the one that flooded and made a mess of the barn."

"He works hard," Edna said, a weariness in her voice that was beyond fatigue. The sunlight streaming through the window sprayed through Edna's graying hair, sparkling on the dark strands, making them seem to move.

The weeks while Lew had been in the Alpena jail had been hard on all of them. Seneca and Twyman had tried to visit Lew, but Sheriff Colfax had refused to let them see him. Then they had come up with the idea of a petition to secure his release. She had ridden all through the hills and up and down the valley to get the signatures. They were all tired. And like Edna, Seneca was worried too, for a different reason. She didn't know what Lew was going to do after he got back home. She wondered if he still had that statement from Clete Sisco, or had the sheriff in Alpena destroyed it? How did Lew feel knowing that Clete too had been murdered? And she had a pretty good idea who had shot that poor man. Shot him in the back.

But she couldn't prove it. And neither could anyone else.

Edna craned her neck to peer up the road where it intersected with the road Twyman would be on when he brought the buggy.

"Oh, here comes Twy," she said.

Seneca saw the horse first; then the buggy came into view. Edna picked up the hatbox. The two women stepped outside. Edna turned to lock the door. Then they both heard something and turned to look in the other direction, toward Alpena.

"Looky there," Edna said, whirling around. Seneca saw them too.

Two riders on horseback streaked across the road and disappeared into the woods on the other side. Those woods bordered Lew's place, three miles of them.

"I saw them," Seneca said.

Twyman had turned the corner and was heading their way, the horse at a fast trot.

"I hope Twy saw them too."

"I think he did."

"And that ain't the first time neither," Edna said.

"What do you mean?"

"I seen 'em when I was taking sun on the front porch today. They rode off across the creek and into the woods over by the cemetery."

"Why didn't you say anything?" Seneca asked.

"I thought they was just two men out hunting or something. Didn't think nothing of it. But them was the same two horses all right."

"Do you know who the riders are?"

Edna shook her head.

"Too far," she said.

Twyman drove the buggy up alongside the front porch, reined in the horse. He had hitched up Red Fox, the fleetest horse in Lew's stable. Three white stockings and a blaze face, Red Fox was all muscle and sinew, stood fifteen hands high, with legs like a Thoroughbred's.

"You see them riders?" Twy said.

Both women nodded.

"They was ridin' hell-bent for leather," Twyman said.

"That's twice today I seen 'em," Edna said.

"I wonder who they are," Twyman said.

Edna scurried off the porch and climbed into the buggy.

"Good-bye, Seneca. See you tomorrow?"

"I'll be here."

"You have a good evenin', Seneca," Twyman said, and clucked to Red Fox. He cracked the reins and the horse started to move.

Edna waved as Twyman turned the buggy and headed for home.

Seneca too wondered who the riders were. They had been too far away to identify, but she had a hunch that Edna had not been wrong about being watched.

That gleam she had seen in the woods when she looked out the back door of the store. It could have come from a telescope or a pair of field glasses.

Someone was watching the store. She was sure of that.

And they were watching Edna too.

Two names came to her mind just then.

Wiley Pope and Fritz Canby.

Who else could it be?

30

LEW TOPPED THE RISE AND SAW THE BUGGY LEAVING THE store. He raised a hand to signal that he was coming, but Twyman was too far away and Lew knew that he wasn't seen. As he put Ruben into a lope, the buggy turned the corner and disappeared. But he saw Seneca walk over to the hitch rail in front of the store and start to loosen the knots on her reins.

"Seneca," Lew called, and kicked Ruben in the flanks, propelling the horse into a full gallop.

Seneca turned around. She lifted a hand to shade her eyes from the sun. Lew waved at her. She waited a moment, as if to be sure who he was, then waved back.

"Lew," she said when he rode up close to her, "I didn't expect you until tomorrow."

"Colfax let me out today. He had to go somewhere tomorrow." Lew was puffing from the exertion of the ride. He swung down from his horse and walked up to Seneca. "God, it's good to see you, Seneca."

She smiled, and her smile was warmer than the sunshine that bathed them in its glow.

"Lew, I'm melting inside. It's so good to see you. So good."

There was an awkward moment; then she lunged at him and wrapped her arms around his waist, hugging him as she lay her head against his chest.

"I've missed you so much, Seneca," he said, his voice laden with a huskiness that betrayed his strong emotions at seeing her, feeling her body against his own.

"I missed you too. I tried to see you. I cried when the sheriff wouldn't let me inside the jail where you were."

She looked up at him. He bowed his head and encircled her waist with his arm, pulling her even tighter against him. He kissed her, knowing he could, knowing he had to and that she wanted him to do that.

"Mmmm," she moaned, and her lips vibrated against his, sending a tingling sensation through his entire body.

"Are you heading home?" he asked when they broke the kiss.

"Yes, I was, but I've got to tell you something, Lew. Something that might be important."

"I know about Clete," he said.

"No, it's something I saw today. Just a little while ago. Two things really."

"What?"

She told him about the flash of light she saw in the woods, then about the two riders crossing the road and disappearing into the woods. She told him about Edna's fears of being watched, and about her concerns over keeping the store's money in her home each night. She told him all this with breathless speed, the words pouring out in a rush, all of them tinged with a sense of urgency.

"Can you show me where those two riders crossed the road?" He pushed her gently away from him.

They rode up the Alpena road a short distance, Seneca in the lead, Lew following. She turned her horse off to the side, staring at the ground.

"Right here," she said. "You can see their tracks."

Lew looked down. He could tell that the horses had been running. Deep track marks surrounded by little clods of dirt plainly showed where the two riders had crossed.

"You go on home, Seneca," Lew said. "I'll see you at the store tomorrow."

"What are you going to do?"

"Follow these tracks. You know who it is, don't you?"

"I know who it might be."

"It's them. I know it is. And they're heading toward my place. And the Butterfields' just beyond."

"Lew, don't you think we ought to go talk to Sheriff Swanson?"

Lew snorted. "Why?"

"He's the law. He could . . ."

"He wears a badge, but he's not the law, any more than Colfax is. I know what he'd say."

"What's that?"

"Swannie would say Wiley and Fritz have every right to ride through the woods."

"I don't know, Lew. Following them could be dangerous."

"Yeah, it could. For them."

He threw a hand up in the air by way of farewell, and rode into the fringe of trees, following the horse tracks. He did not look back and see Seneca lift her hand in a futile attempt to wave good-bye to him.

The tracks were easy to follow for the first hundred yards. After that, the riders had slowed and were seemingly picking their way over sodden dead leaves, over hardpan, through dense thickets. Lew felt some admiration for the way they tried to conceal their trail.

The sun was falling lower in the sky. The light was changing the closer he got to the ridges where the tracks led him. He began to see the dazzling white lights of the dogwoods blooming. They had flowered while he was in jail, and here and there he saw the familiar rosy petals of the redbuds, splashes of color against the cedars. The oaks were leafing out too, and he could not see very far ahead.

There was the scent of spring in the air, and at any other time, he would have enjoyed the ride through the greening sylvan glades with their emerald carpets of fresh grass.

Lew made a decision as the slanted rays of the sun began to draw away, bring out the shadows, make dark puddles beneath the trees, change the composition of every object. Light still played through the weak green of new leaves in the higher branches, but below, shadows seeped from every rock and tree, and the tracks were fading out as if they had been erased or smudged over with charcoal.

He knew where Wiley and Fritz were going. Not to his place, but beyond, to where the Butterfields lived in the embrace of a wide hollow. He did not know how far ahead the two killers were, but he knew he had to beat them to Twyman's because they were up to no good. They were not riding through the woods because they liked the hard going. They were there because they did not want to be seen. The woods were a perfect hiding place, and they could ride straight to Twyman's place, come up behind the house, and he and Edna would never see them until it was too late.

Lew turned his horse to the road, and once he left the woods, he spurred Ruben into a gallop. He rode into the setting sun, blinded by the golden lances of light, hoping he could get to Twyman's before the sun completely set. But as he passed his place, the sky was ablaze with light flung upward from below the horizon, and some of the clouds that had raged red and yellow moments before were turning to ashen relics, turning into murky gray smoke.

By the time Lew reached the end of the road and turned up the lane to Twyman's, the darkness had filled the hollow and smoothed down the ridges, softened all the treetops into a blurred skyline. And the darkness began to swallow the land.

Lew felt as if he was riding into a deep, dark cave.

And inside the cave, he knew, in the deepest parts, fearsome dragons lurked.

Wiley and Fritz.

Just before he reached the nearly invisible house buried deep in the shadows of night, Lew heard a piercing scream.

A woman's scream, and it ripped through him like a saber, cutting his nerves to shreds, knotting his stomach up with coils of freezing steel cables that tightened with every breath.

Lew leaped from Ruben when he reached the front gate and hit the ground running, pistol in hand.

Edna screamed again.

31

THE WINDOWS GLOWED A PALE ORANGE FROM THE COAL-OIL lamps.

"Where's the damned money?" Wiley's voice, loud, threatening.

The front door gaped open. Shadows moving inside like spectral figures flung against a cave wall by dancing firelight.

"Leave her alone," Twyman gruffed from inside the house.

Lew leaped onto the porch and burst through the front door, hunched over, holding his cocked pistol at hip level.

He took in the scene with a single glance. Twyman lay on the floor, blood streaming from his face. Fritz stood over him, a six-gun in his hand, ready to bring it down again in another smashing blow. Wiley had Edna by the throat, throttling her so that she could no longer scream. Her dress was torn and there were open slashes on her face, wounds that oozed with blood. Wiley held a pistol in his right hand and there was blood smeared on the blued barrel.

On the table between the front room and the kitchen sat a large hatbox, strangely incongruous in the very center of the dining room.

Fritz swung his pistol to aim it at Lew.

Lew squeezed the trigger of his Colt, felt it buck in his hand. The powder exploded in the cartridge, shooting lead and fire from the muzzle. The bullet caught Fritz square in the gut. He doubled over in pain, his eyes wide and rolling in their sockets. His fingers went slack and his pistol slipped from his grasp and fell to the floor, making a dull thud on the rug.

"You sonofabitch," Wiley yelled. His left hand dropped away from Edna's throat and she collapsed into a heap on the floor.

Wiley brought his pistol up and fired at Lew, his mouth twisted in a tight grimace. His pistol roared and spat fire like a dragon's breath.

Lew felt the whoosh of air next to his ear as the bullet sizzled past him.

He cocked the single-action Colt again and fired point-blank at Wiley. Then he hammered back again as he charged forward, his anger a towering explosion inside him, bursting in his eardrums louder than the bark of his pistol.

Lew's bullet smashed into Wiley's chest, high, near the shoulder bone. Lew could hear the crunch and snap of bone as the bullet struck it. Wiley twisted to one side, his face contorted in pain. He brought his pistol up again, but his arm seemed limp and uncoordinated, like a puppet's arm when the strings go slack.

"Bastard," Wiley said as one leg began to collapse.

Lew barreled into him and smashed him across the face with the barrel of his Colt.

"How does that feel, you sonofabitch?" Lew spat as Wiley crumpled and landed on his butt. Lew kicked his pistol from his hand and laid into him again with a cracking blow across Wiley's nose. Blood spewed from both nostrils and welled up in a cut across the bridge. Again, the sound of crunching bone. Wiley fell back, but he still held onto his pistol.

Lew stepped back as Wiley tried to bring the pistol up. He groaned from the effort, but the pistol kept rising.

It took only seconds for Lew to think it through. He held a man's life in his hands. Wiley would probably survive the wound in his chest. He might even be arrested and go to trial. But would any of that happen in Carroll County?

"Justice," Lew whispered as he took deadly aim, the barrel of his pistol pointed right at the center of Wiley's forehead.

A blank look registered on Wiley's face for just that instant before Lew squeezed the trigger. His lips moved to form a word he would never utter.

Lew squeezed the trigger, and the Colt belched death in a streaming comet of fire and lead.

A black hole appeared in the middle of Wiley's face, just above and between his eyebrows. Light fled from his eyes and his pistol clattered to the floor as he crumpled into a lifeless heap.

The stench of him filled the air as his bowels moved in one last spasm.

It was then that buck fever gripped Lew and he began to tremble. He had taken the lives of two men, all in the incredible twinkling of an eye. He had stepped across a threshold and now stood on the edge of a terrible precipice. He could not go back, and there was a widening chasm in front of him. Beyond that moment lay the unknown future, an unknown land. If he stepped wrong, he would fall a long way. He would fall to his death perhaps.

He heard Edna whimpering, sobbing.

Twyman scrambled to his feet, but Lew stood there, in a trance, overcome by the awesome specter of death that rose up inside him, enveloping the anger and hate until it was nearly extinguished.

"You said something, Lew," Twyman said as he came up behind Lew and put a hand on his shoulder. "What was it you said?"

"I don't remember," Lew said.

He looked down at Wiley's face. The eyes were wide-open, sightless, staring at some distant point beyond human comprehension. They were glazing over with the chill frost of death, like a deer's eyes except for the evil that still seemed to pulsate from within the dead hulk that once was Wiley Pope.

"He said, 'Justice,' Twy," Edna said as Twyman helped her to her feet. "That's what he said. I heard it plain as day."

"Well, I'm damned," Twyman said.

Lew slipped his pistol back in his holster. He felt dazed, but oddly exhilarated, as if he had come to the end of a long journey and found something of value inside a cave filled with grotesque creatures, demons from the very depths of hell.

He knew he had crossed over into another world and that he might never be able to return to the one he had left behind.

Wiley and Fritz were both dead.

But Virgil Pope was still alive. So was Luke Canby, Fritz's father.

Sheriff Billy Jim Colfax was alive too.

And so was the law that had failed Lew.

But so too was the law Lew now had. This was his law in a lawless land.

The law of the gun.

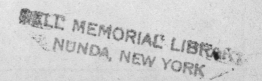

Spur Award-Winning Author

Jory Sherman

Texas Dust

When Joby Redmond returned from war,
he thought he had put the killing
behind him. But when his lifelong
enemy appears—and begins terrorizing
the Redmond family—Joby knows
the fight is far from over.

0-425-19430-2

Available wherever books are sold or at
penguin.com

Spur Award-Winning Author

Jory Sherman

Blood River

Reeling from the murder of the girl he loved, young Chip Morgan seeks a new beginning in Colorado. But when he finds no succor, only more bloodshed, he begins a quest for vengeance that leads him to a place where youthful recklessness turns to true grit.

"JORY SHERMAN IS A NATIONAL TREASURE."
—LOREN D. ESTLEMAN

"ONE OF THE PREMIERE STORYTELLERS
OF THE AMERICAN WEST."
—DON COLDSMITH

0-425-19991-6

Available wherever books are sold or at penguin.com

PETER BRANDVOLD

DEALT THE DEVIL'S HAND 0-425-18731-4

With a bloodthirsty posse prepared to pump him
full of hot lead, bounty hunter Lou Prophet tries
to steer clear of the sweet young thing who's
making him think twice about his drifter lifestyle.

THE DEVIL AND LOU PROPHET 0-425-18399-8

Call him manhunter, tracker, or bounty hunter.
Lou Prophet loved his work—it kept him in wine
and women, and was never dull. His latest job
sounds particularly attractive: he's to escort to
the courthouse a showgirl who's a prime
witness in a murder trial. But some very
dangerous men are moving in to make sure the
pair never reach the courthouse alive.

**AVAILABLE WHEREVER BOOKS ARE SOLD OR AT
PENGUIN.COM**

(Ad #B412)